FOREWORD

When 'New Fiction' ceased publishing there was much wailing and gnashing of teeth, the showcase for the short story had offered an opportunity for practitioners of the craft to demonstrate their talent.

Phoenix-like from the ashes. 'New Fiction' has risen with the sole purpose of bringing forth new and exciting short stories from new and exciting writers.

The art of the short story writer has been practised from ancient days, with many gifted writers producing small, but hauntingly memorable stories that linger in the imagination.

I believe this selection of stories will leave echoes in your mind for many days. Read on and enjoy the pleasure of that most perfect form of literature, the short story.

Parvus Est Bellus.

CONTENTS

A DAY TO REMEMBER
Joe McGowan

(Just because our prayers aren't always answered immediately doesn't mean that no one's listening)

'A cup of tea, son?' A pleasantly delivered question, falling on unheeding ears. 'Matthew?'

The slightly impatient, more forceful, tone of the second discharge of dialogue was sufficient to penetrate the consciousness of the young man.

'Oh, yes, ehrm . . . sorry, what did you say?'
'I said,' (far more impatiently this time) 'would-you-like-a-cup-of-tea?'
'Yeah, sure. Thanks. I wasn't thinking, Annie, sorry.'

Matthew *was* thinking, very intensely, but not about anything remotely connected with his immediate surroundings.

The stooped, white-haired little figure, aided (though not significantly) by a walking stick, hobbled off in the direction of the kitchen, muttering discontentedly as she burned up the inches of her journey.

At that moment Matthew was assaulted by guilt. His gran was, how old now? (To his continuing frustration he now couldn't even recall that – was he going mad?) . . . and he hadn't even shown her the basic courtesy of attentiveness. Added to which, she was off to make tea for *him,* a grown man in his thirties.

He launched himself off his gran's second favourite armchair – seriously dishevelling the two patterned cushions upon which he had been nestling –
must fix those before she sees them
and within seconds was solemnly following on behind the old woman's slow, processional walk towards the teapot.

'I think I might have a migraine coming on, Annie.' (An affectionate rendering of *Annabella.*) 'My head's felt weird, sort of numb, since this morning - even after my walk earlier on. That's the reason – *one* of the reasons – why I popped round.'

Annie never cared much for the idea that her relatives would come to see her with anything other than the unselfish intention of checking on her well-being, so one had to be careful about declaring particular motivations for a visit.

'Oh, you know *I'll* always be here, son,' (a barely disguised quip that no one comes to take her out much these days) 'you didn't have to worry about that. And you're probably just working too hard on that compuser of yours.'

'Computer,' he corrected – knowing full well there was little chance of her complying. Even though they had been commonplace items for many years now, to his gran's generation computers were still the experimental and luxurious toys of an inferior age destined for self-destruction.

Predictably, Annie did not acknowledge his correction, and instead adopted the position of an optometrist. 'They're bad for your eyes, you know. You mark my words, in another ten years from now there'll be twice as many people wearing glasses – or stone *blind!'* She punctuated the last word disdainfully; eyes magnified behind the lenses of her own little gold rimmed spectacles.

The grandson attempted to offer some assistance towards preparing the tea or laying the table, but was promptly dismissed by a resolute waving gesture from the veteran tea-maker, indicating that he should be seated at the kitchen table.

Annie had grown accustomed to living alone now, and often displayed a neurotic distrust of anyone's ability to perform every day task in her home – which included the positioning of cushions on an armchair.

'. . . on top of all that, it's now starting to feel like I've lost something – or forgotten, maybe. I don't know. I haven't a clue what it is.' Matthew continued the endeavour to explain his banal cerebral condition while his gran, now sitting at the kitchen table also, drained her second cup of tea and watched him studiously with those still clear and youthful looking blue eyes. 'Things haven't been right with me for hours,' he added despondently.

In fact, ever since that morning, when he had sat in his bedroom staring blankly at the PC monitor, things had not been 'right' with Matthew. He had tried to let the words flit naturally into his mind, the way you're supposed to, but they remained elusive; lost and yet, paradoxically, ever-present – for they were always there *somewhere*, challenging all comers to play their infuriating game of hide-and-seek where the story teller is always *IT*. Like a masochistic navigator of his own emotions, Matthew had steered his way through the disappointment, impatience, frustration and, ultimately, rage when the mental block became complete – his final desperation manifesting itself in the form of a brief but sincere prayer for assistance which he mouthed silently; eyes closed.

'. . . *is yours now and forever, Amen.*'

But the words he was searching for kept themselves hidden; all the time giggling and mocking his devout offering.

It was then that Matthew had left the room and his house for fear of what he might do to the innocent third party – the computer screen.

'It's really strange, Annie. I feel as though I'm drugged, or that all my consciousness has somehow sunk *deeper* inside my body, or . . . or something's preventing me from thinking properly. And yet it's all more subtle than that.'

It *was* rather more subtle than that. For the last two hours or more in Annie's flat it had seemed to Matthew like he was viewing the world through a subliminal veil of gauze; imperceptible to the naked eye, yet frustratingly obvious to the subconscious. There was no headache – yet – but a comparable discomfort caused by his invalided senses which was both unnerving and ominous. And contained within the tenacious, heavy fog that had descended upon his brain was some kind of memory anaesthetic.

'I just *know* I've forgotten something. I sense it's big and I should be remembering it – like an important birthday, or an appointment . . .' (then, after a thoughtful pause) . . . 'It's there, whatever it is, but just tormentingly out of reach.' (Just like *the words* this morning,

Matthew?) 'Dear God, this could drive you to distraction – or bloody insanity.'

It was noticeable that Annie had remained uncharacteristically quiet during this sincere oration – even more noticeable that Matthew had not been reprimanded for his 'language' – when normally by this time she would have interjected with at least a couple of rebuttals or well-informed opinions. And when he looked up to see his confidant somewhat distractedly rubbing at an invisible stain on her floral patterned pinafore, Matthew could only feel further dispirited – not to mention a little hurt.

'Maybe I'm coming down with something?' he quizzically suggested, scanning the endearing lines and wrinkles on the wizened old face for some spark of comprehension. Nothing. 'Of course, I could be dying.' Not even a raised eyebrow. *Now* who wasn't paying attention?

'You've always enjoyed ghost stories, Matthew. I thought I'd give you something that might interest you. Maybe you can even use it for your next story, or one of those competitions you like to enter.'

Matthew, now even more disgruntled at Annie's apparent dismissal of his ailment, could only wait in perplexed aggravation for enlightenment as to what the 'something' was. But the seconds went on and there was no response. His gran only rather furtively continued to wipe at the phantom imperfection on her pinafore, eyes downcast all the while.

He had just opened his mouth to speak when she launched back into life again. 'That reminds me, here . . .' (tossing a newspaper with surprise force – but predictable inaccuracy – across the table towards him) . . . 'there's a story in there about a man in Dalmarnock who's got ghosts in his house.'

The story was not especially interesting or, for that matter, particularly credible. The full page article included a large black and white photograph of a forlorn-looking elderly man holding a broken ornament which, the report claimed, had been smashed in a frenzy of poltergeist activity that has been *'plaguing the hitherto peaceful life of pensioner Steven Mitchell, 76, for nearly two months'*.

'Interesting,' was the only response that indulgence would allow Matthew when he had read the piece.

'Take the newspaper home with you, as a little reminder,' Annie insisted – obviously far more convinced of the article's potential for yielding a decent story than her favourite grandson (the part-time auto mechanic and budding writer) was.

Stirring another sugar distractedly into his cup, Matthew conceded that whilst tea was on the menu, sympathy, apparently, was not.

For the remainder of the visit, Matthew gave Annie the undivided attention of his eyes while his mind journeyed through vast expanses of personal preoccupation and speculation; nodding at intervals or offering the occasional affirming *'Mmmhh,'* whenever intuition prompted him to do so.

Annie walked with him - as she always had with her visitors – to the lift situated on the landing just outside her small rented high-rise flat.

The lift had conveniently alighted, as though waiting for him, at the fifth floor – his gran's level.

Clutching the newspaper, he pressed the small black operating button and the lift rattled into noisy existence; its corrugated aluminium door sliding open sideways.

'Thanks for the tea,' Matthew said dutifully.

Annie stepped forward and hugged him. An unusually overt display of affection for her.

'Look, I only live down the road, I'll be back soon,' he reminded her in an incredulous but consoling tone. *Some days she can feel quite sorry for herself, so you have to walk on egg shells,* the independent grown up inside him said. But the eternal grandson within exuberantly retorted, *I love my granny, Annie.*

She smiled.

The image remained in his mind long after the lift doors had closed and he had descended to ground level.

That same image dwelt in his mind two weeks later as he typed the final words of the story. He wanted to truly thank Annie for the tale she had given him, and for removing his writer's block in the process, but that was impossible.

The sadness was rekindled with each letter Matthew transferred from keyboard to monitor; the sense of unfulfillable longing that he had felt on the day of Annie's funeral was once again revived; the unspoken words and sentiments that would remain forever mute were vividly recalled – all accompanied by a single, overwhelming regret. But there was much gratitude too – both for the story, which had become a legacy, *and* the newspaper; that special souvenir of a day to remember.

Even before he had typed a single word, Matthew knew there could only be one title for the story.

A Day to Remember.

A precious day, unwittingly taken for granted in the manner so quintessential to human nature.

An impossible day, when he had taken tea with his gran and struggled with an intimidating mind paralysis, so powerful and mysterious it had somehow caused him to forget something very important . . .

. . . that he had attended Annie's funeral three years previous.

TIME TO CHANGE
K F Lainton

The guns were almost deafening in their roar. Trenches were waist high in water. The clay soil held the water and with 115 men in 200 yards of trench the conditions were almost unbelievably bad. The German advance had been unexpected. After 14 weeks of almost no movement of either army, the lines had seemed frozen. Last night's breakthrough had caught the Canadian unit in a virtually indefensible position. It could only be a matter of time before the sheer weight of numbers annihilated them.

Mal did not want to die. Yes, he had volunteered. His work as a geologist had come to a convenient stage at the University and he could take a break for a few months. After all everyone had said the war would all be over in six months.

Now the realisation that he would never have a chance to analyse another rock sample filled him with almost unbearable sadness.

To know, without any chance of escape, that your position was about to be overrun, was as near to living a nightmare as Mal had ever come. His mind was suddenly wrenched back to the present by the almost instantaneous appearance of a large semi-spherical machine in front of him. He threw himself flat in the mud, assuming that the enemy had devised some yet more fiendish engine of war. It was a full minute before he lifted his head and looked up. He rose slowly and carefully approached the semi-sphere. As he got near a screen defined itself on the side. A friendly voice, female, with a home-town sound greeted him.
Hi', it said.
'Who's in charge here?'

Mal ran at the fastest speed that a crowded trench position would allow. His particular point on the defence line meant that he alone would have seen the arrival of the device.

Mal had difficulty in deciding exactly how he should explain what he had seen. When he was face-to-face with Major Collins the words which came out were almost as much a surprise to him as to the Major.

'I think I've found a way out for us, Major. You had better come with me and see this for yourself.'

Collins had always assessed Mal as a reliable and sensible member of the unit. He knew Mal was a geologist and thought that some hidden cave could have been discovered. He made his decision immediately. 'Benson, Komanski come with me. Rogers, take over here.'

When Collins found the screen he was as completely amazed as Mal had been a few minutes earlier.

'What the hell is that?' he demanded.
Mal was saved from a reply by the screen flickering to life again.

'Hi' said the voice - not quite in the same tone as before.

'I'm here to take you on a trip. Where would you like to go?'

'Anywhere but here,' growled Collins.

'OK' answered the screen.
'I'll open up.'

Silently a door opened. Bright lights screamed out.

Collins jerked his head to Komanski. They took a side of the door each.

'Benson cover us. You too,' to Mal.

Collins' head appeared out of the door. A big grin spread over his face.

'You've got to see this. Come on it's OK.'

Benson hung back but Mal's curiosity was fully aroused. He went in and noted that Benson was following but only slowly.

What he saw was amazing. After the squalor of the trenches, a comfortable room. The contrast made the light comfortable furniture looks like paradise.

A new screen, much larger than the last glowed into life.

'Hi, I'm glad to welcome you here. How many of you are going to come aboard?'

Collins considered.

'There are 115 of us here but when are you planning on going?'

'You can go anytime you like,' intonated the screen.

'What kind of a vehicle is this?'
It was Komanski whose low growl of a question contrasted with the high sweet voice from the screen.

Before anyone could venture a guess, the screen answered
'Maybe you'd like to see what will happen here in one hour.'

The screen flashed again and they all saw the familiar terrain in front of them. The enemy were advancing at a considerable pace and Mal had the quite uncanny experience of seeing himself shot as the enemy crossed the position's inner perimeter. The slaughter was brief, efficient and total. When it was finished all four viewers had seen themselves shot and watched their own death agonies, as well as those of every other soldier in the unit.

The sweet voice continued.
'Of course you can stay if you wish to. That is the future as it will unfold unless you change it.'

'How can we change the future?' It was Mal who asked.

'Anyone on board before take off will have a different future.'

Collins had the military training to know that in the face of total surprise any decision was better than no decision. He had also sufficient humanity to have hated watching the slaughter of the men of his unit.

'We are all coming aboard,' he snapped.

Orders were quickly given. The assembling of 115 men, even allowing for a series of shots being fired across the whole line of the trench was a matter of less than 7 minutes.

As the last man entered, the door closed and nobody on board was aware of any motor as the semi-sphere disappeared from the view of anyone who had been watching.

Nobody was watching.

Intermission.

The advance met no resistance. The position was occupied without a shot being fired. The German commander reported a total victory with no prisoners taken. That would be much better for his promotion than to report that the defenders had escaped his encircling forces and nobody had seen them go or could find out their escape route.

The journey seemed to take a week. Everyone found a sort of paradise. No gun fire. Showers, excellent food. Abundant drink. Personalised entertainment in small side booths. Films; music; strange new sensations. If a viewer sat in one of the chairs and watched a film, his arms could be rested on conventionally shaped chair arms. In that position the viewer not only saw and heard but was actually part of the action viewed. Smells, sensations, everything was experienced at first hand. If the arms were raised, the sensations stopped.

Collins had spent a lot of time during the first hours of the journey at a console. It was, the sweet voice had told them, the only control necessary.

'You merely set the date and time you want and I will take you there.'

It had taken some time before Collins had accepted the idea of a time machine and that he was in one. He demanded of Mal - who had been designated in charge of scientific matters - whether such a thing was possible and how come it was taking so long.

'If we are travelling in time, how long will it take?'

Mal had expressed doubts about the concept of time travel but when pressed had said that he had thought if such a thing were possible, movement from one point in time to another would be instantaneous. He thought for a while and then said.

'I suppose it could be like a railway. You get on at one point and then out at another - and the journey itself takes time.'

The unit all noticed certain strange things. Although they had the sensation of days passing, each had a great sense of relaxation and peace. On the seventh day of the journey Mal called the Major to the console. The day they had fixed on the digital choice touch screen was the time they wished to go to, had been 3 years forward. They were sure that the war would be over by then and that they could all go home to peace.

However the dial was now suddenly moving at an incredible rate. Not days but years were flashing past on the digital touch screen. No action they could take could stop the rate of change.

Change.

'You have arrived safely. The year is 2915,' said the sweet voice.

Collins demanded to know why they had not gone forward the 3 years they had requested, rather than a thousand years.

'I'm sorry,' said the sweet voice, 'the year was pre-programmed before I took off from here.'

The door opened. As they looked out they could see over 300 other semi-spherical domes of the same type they had travelled in.

From each group of travellers were pouring. The faces of the nearest group looked strained and puzzled.

As each vehicle emptied, the door closed and the vehicle vanished.

A huge screen flashed up at the side of the launching field.

To experienced soldiers, the unmistakable sounds of a battle being fought nearby brought a sudden tension of nerves.

A voice boomed over the area.
'This position is under serious threat of being overrun by the enemy,' it announced.

'Weapons will be issued to all of you freshly arrived recruits and you should prepare for a final defence of this position in one hour.
Thank you for volunteering. Your sacrifice will be remembered.'

MISS MISERICORD AND THE SCRAMBLED EGGHEADS - A FARCE
Alexandra Walker

'Hello, Cracker. You're always the first.' Georgina vigorously shook the rain from her umbrella outside in the corridor before entering the schoolroom.

'Hi, Georgie,' Cracker nodded to his favourite colleague. He had been nicknamed Cracker after the television series.
'My mother used to take me to lots of January sales when I was a boy. Got into the habit of queuing up to be first in.'

'Ha, ha!'

'I thought you might be old miseryguts,' Claude, the French lecturer submitted.

'Have you noticed how names often fit the person? I used to work for someone called J P Court - he became a judge. And then there was Peter Ferguson - be came a television . . . actor.'

'I had a friend called Robert Soul; he became an idiot.'

Georgina giggled.
'Ssssh! Here she comes. She wouldn't appreciate that last one.' They heard the sturdy clip-clop of matronly shoes.

'Brown leather lace-ups?' Cracker had his back to the door.

'You're right,' Georgina peered at the shoes as they came into room A15 and noisily clumped across the plain wooden floor to their regular seat next to the radiator.
'But then you are the psychologist.'

'Morning everyone,' Miss Misericord dumped her bag on a desk and scraped back the red plastic seat.

Cracker gritted his teeth. He was forever telling off his students for doing that but he could hardly criticise a fellow teacher.
'Good morning, Margaret,' he politely responded. It was the only way you could talk to her; she had no sense of humour.

'There's nothing good about it,' she almost snapped. 'It's raining. My car's playing up. I've got my worst group this morning for three-and-a-half solid hours. *And* I have to listen to Charles droning on for this hour. What do these meetings achieve? We'll all get a piece of paper in a week's time telling us what's been decided, whether we're here or not.'

By the time Charlie entered the room, three more people had arrived, making up the entire academic section.
'Good morning everyone,' Charlie put on a cheery smile as he entered the room, dropping his pile of papers unceremoniously onto the main desk.
'Lovely fresh weather, isn't it?'

'If you're a duck.'

'Ooh! That *was* original, Kwacker,' Georgina smirked.

Charlie ignored the badinage and a quick glance around the group assured him they would all be happy to move on.

'I'll dispense with the minutes of the last meeting, unless anyone has a real problem with that?'

'Let's just get on with it, shall we Charles?' Margaret waved her hand as though to dismiss any objections.

He gave her an impatient glance.
'The reason I called you all urgently together was the whole future of the academic section,' he said sombrely. 'You've all heard he rumours; we've been progressively underfunded, we're not advertised sufficiently, our numbers are going down.'

'Yes, we've all felt the results of the management's cuts in our section,' Paul, the science teacher complained.

'That's because the Principal, and the management team, of course,' Charlie added sarcastically, 'want to expand computer studies, the special needs sections, and vocational sections, and not the academic section. Fewer and fewer people are studying academic subjects, here at any rate, and we're seen as too expensive. As you know, it's been the policy for a few years to only run courses with a minimum of twelve people. We're currently down to an average of nine per class and the trend in most sections is to go down each year. So, for example, your sociology A-level course, Georgina, may start with twelve, it did last year I believe but, with drop-outs you end with only five or six taking the exam. And most of the other sections are the same.'

'All that's partly the influence of the New Right and Mrs Thatcher. She didn't like historians or sociologists so my departments were both allowed to run down and, of course, government and politics was 'done in' two years ago. It's a countrywide phenomenon, not just our problem here. It's the age of vocationalism - training, not education,' Georgina offered, sociologically.

'That's another reason why the Principal sees our department as too expensive to keep open. And that's the crux. The word is the academic department is to be run down and course closed wherever possible. We're expendable, it seems.'

'We've been expendable for the last decade; they haven't advertised our department properly for years,' one of the English lecturers said emphatically.

'I really don't see how we're seen as 'too expensive'. We don't cost much at all, only in salaries. But that's the same for all departments. We have very little extras each year and the students pay for their own books,' the business studies lecturer voiced a general grievance.

'So, does this mean some of us are out of a job next September?' Cracker asked, jocularly, but with serious intent.

'Some of you might be, though I think you might survive, Cracker,' Charlie responded honestly, but nervously before dropping his bombshell: 'We're going to offer the evening courses as usual, but the day A-levels have all been cancelled. We will no longer be running these.'

A stunned silence followed his announcement. For a moment no one could find anything to say. It was so brutal, so unexpected that they hadn't understood for a few seconds. Then the storm broke.

'Hold on a minute, Charlie, are you telling us that none of us will have any work next year other than evening classes?'

Charlie looked hangdog.

'That's about the size of it, Cracker. With, perhaps a few GCSE lessons.'

Charlie was fundamentally a 'nice' guy but he couldn't handle these occasions. He would never rise higher than lower-middle-management because he lacked the killer instinct. He felt their anger and disappointment and worry for their futures as much as they did themselves.

'But my classes haven't been that small; I've never had less than fifteen. Why are my classes being cut?'

'Policy, old chap. No point in offering just psychology if they can't take any other subjects alongside it.'

'Same with English. We've always been well attended . . . '

'According to the figures for the last five years,' he consulted his notes, 'there's been a steady drop in *retention* of your students which has led to an average of ten students in your classes. You might all start off in September with around twelve or fifteen students, but the fallout is high. You all know under twelve students is simply not cost-effective any more.'

'And cost-effectiveness rules the education system,' the business studies lecturer remarked sourly.

'Mrs Thatcher and the New Right again. Cost effectiveness, competition, league tables . . .'

'Oh, shut up about that grocer's daughter. I don't want to hear that woman's name again. She's wrecked the education system. Our part of it, anyway,' the normally conservative Margaret snapped at Georgina, knowing her classes were down to only four or five students and she would be out of work before September.

'Don't I know it,' Georgina nodded.

'Do you mean to say there won't be any English A-level lessons either?'

'Not during the daytime. As I said, the evening classes will be available, providing enough people enrol in them from the beginning.'

'And what is 'enough' students? Twelve? Fifteen?'

Charlie avoided looking at the English lecturer. He had rather fancied his chances with her. He was only in his thirties and she was just out of college. No chance now, though, he thought.

'I don't know yet. They haven't given me the details. I'm not even sure I should be telling you this until next week, but I'm affected too. If your sections go, my job as department head goes too.'

'If our sections go . . . do you mean some or all of us might not have *any* teaching work from September?'

Charlie paused for a fraction too long.

'This is preposterous!' Margaret burst out. 'Whoever heard of an educational institution without any education? They surely can't do this? What does the funding council have to say about it all? Don't they have rules covering what's taught here?'

'I don't know yet, Margaret. I have a meeting with the senior management team next week and I'll ask all the questions you put to me. But I can't answer them until then.'

'Can I get back to basics?' Cracker asked, patiently, but with a note of anger in his voice. 'Take a hypothetical situation. Suppose I have *no* classes, A-level or GCSE. What are my options then?'

'As I see it, you have three options: you can find other work, take redundancy, or perhaps, if you're lucky, take up a part-time contract.'

'How much would the redundancy package consist of?'

'I don't know yet. That's something I want to know for myself, obviously.'

'Could I take redundancy and still take a part-time contract, assuming one was available?'

'You can still work part-time, even if you're made redundant,' the union representative chipped in.
'What would the union have to say about this?' Charlie asked her.

'I'll find out and let you know next week. I assume you'll call a meeting next week to let us know what your meeting turns up, Charlie?'

There was silence for a few moments as they each inwardly digested the fate which awaited them. Faced with the imminent demise of their entire department and being thrown out of work, with dependants at home to feed and clothe, and mortgages to pay, there were few reactions open to them: dejection, fear for their futures, anger, frustration, or even hysteria. Their carefully nurtured world was collapsing around their ears. They were rational, reasonable human beings but for most of them hysteria in one form or another seemed to be the only viable option; and for these academics, hysteria took the form of sarcasm or cynical laughter.

'This has got to be some kind of a joke,' Georgie suggested to Cracker, half smiling. 'It isn't April the first, is it?'

Margaret glanced at Georgina over the half-spectacles perched on the end of her nose.
'This isn't a joke, you know!'

Georgina felt reprimanded in front of the group and half-angrily, half-jokingly responded: 'No. It's no yolk.'

'Eggsactly!' said Cracker, quickly picking up Georgie's frame of mind.

'Well, it seems to me that this brain-drain of the academic section is eggsactly what happens to eggheads,' Cracker's neighbour added, passing the baton to his female colleague from business studies.

'You're a bit hard-boiled about it all, aren't you?'

'I thought she was being rather a good egg, personally.' The banter passed from one lecturer to another.

'I think you poached my line' Charlie added, a tiny smile playing around his mouth, despite the desperation he, and he knew, everyone in the room felt. If it helped release their tension, who was he to stop them playing out a scene from Alice in Wonderland.

'I don't know about you all, but I could do with some chips to go with all these eggs,' the last person in the room added, running out of ideas.

Margaret looked from one to the other over her half-glasses, a puzzled and increasingly annoyed frown flittering across her forehead. Finally she couldn't stand it any longer and burst out:
'Well! I must say in view of what Charles has told us this morning, your reactions are absolutely nonsensical. I think the combination of bad weather and bad news has scrambled your brains!'

At the other end of the corridor, the Principal paused in his dictation to his secretary as the sound of raucous laughter, loud, continuous and hysterical, reached his office. Aware that Charles was probably giving the academic section at least a hint of the bad news, laughter was the least expected response. His body tensed in anticipation of some unforeseen action from his lecturers.
'Jean, would you just nip along to A15 and see what that was all about?'

After a few moments she returned.

'Well?'

'Cracker said to tell you that Margaret Misericord just made a joke.'

'Ah!' The Principal responded, relaxing. 'Now I understand.'

UP THE BOLEEN
Don Ferguson

It was a cold bright day with a keen wind stinging our faces as we four boys met at a prearranged corner of an east end street. Our short trousers, customary then, did little to protect our legs from becoming chapped by the cold, but around our necks we proudly wore long, knitted scarves, striped in the colours of our local football team. These afforded an insulating warmth while displaying to all around where our loyalties lay.

Lenny, Jock and Georgie were patiently waiting until I finally joined them breathless and finishing the remains of toast from my breakfast. It was Saturday. A day of freedom and untold expectations. No school for two whole days. Two whole days! We were boys on the loose, away from the restricted timetables of school and seized with the desire to run wild seeking adventure. Our hearts were young and excitement lifted our steps as we raced along the streets, laughing and giggling while heading for the centre of town.

Pushing and shoving each other like gamboling animals we felt a thrill of anticipation for the coming afternoon football match. West Ham at home. This is what we had been waiting for. Nearing the road which was a junction, with one of them leading off to the main centre of the town we became suddenly aware of a football landing in our midst followed by a voice yelling out to us to kick it back!

And there across the other side of the road was a boy we called Abo fiercely indicating that we were to pass the ball back to him. Abecrombie or better known to us all as Abo was to be instantly obeyed. He possessed the requisite 'leader of the pack' something that influenced boys of our age.

Following his demand, Lenny leapt onto the ball and expertly flicked it back across the road to him. Alongside Abo raced another boy named Tuck, short for Tucker who followed Abo like his shadow, very rarely speaking but able to run, kick and dribble a ball like an experienced player. It was said that in a year or so he would be turning out for the Juniors so despite his brooding silence we regarded him with reservations.

These two boys lived more than half a dozen streets away from us almost bordering on the next district of Plaistow which in our eyes made them strangers, so much did we preserve local territorial customs.

By now, the six of us were engaged in a wild passing game of football across the street, kicking the ball from side to side, prompting angry looks and responses from some people as they busily hurried along to shop in the centre of town.

'You boys should take that ball to the park and play there!' A man in a bowler hat irately shouted to us, dodging the ball as it sailed close over his head.

'They should be stopped! Call the police!' A woman angrily snapped, her face grim with outrage. Her threatening comments prompted ridiculing laughter from us as we galloped on towards our destination which was commonly known as the 'Boleen'. It was an old weathered public house with wooden floors covered with sawdust and on Saturday afternoons when a football game was to be played, filled to the brim with men with a thirst, fighting their way to the bar to be served before they rushed away to see the match.

Next to the public house was a castle. The Boleyn Castle where it was said that Henry the Eighth in the days of his reign came to visit his Ann Boleyn and then would go riding on their horses as far as Wanstead 'along the way'. In our small young world, everything of importance took place here.

The wireless told us of another world far away where there were dictators stirring up lots of trouble, but that was for others to worry about. Our world was here. Our domain. Nothing else mattered then.

Very soon trams packed with supporters would come to the Boleyn corner, clatter to a halt on silver rails and then disgorge men in large bustling numbers on to a crowded pavement. Next door to this public house was the Boleyn cinema, down at heel and in need of repair. There, afternoon screen performances would commence with audiences filling it to capacity, bringing with them their lunch, usually of fish and chips, followed by an orange or banana, so by the time the first film was showing, pungent aromas of partly consumed food would float overhead on the auditorium air.

'We're going for pie and mash,' Lenny came back to tell us after he had agreed this with Abo and Tucker.

'We're not!' I said defiantly, in answer to his announcement. 'We're going to the corner caff. That's right Dennis? Georgie? Yes, that's right!' I exclaimed without a reply from either of them. That Lenny should desert us for those two interlopers Abo and Tucker miffed me. They're not in our gang!

Once inside the cafe and warmed by the body heat of the crowd inside and the mug of hot tea and a cheesecake topped with coconut shreds, the notion of Lenny deserting us for the other side soon evaporated.

It was now mid-morning and around us on the streets young children played with whips and tops, iron hoops that let off sparks, marbles perilously played in the gutters and scooters that whizzed by with roller skaters weaving through all of them. Everywhere was bursting with life. Street vendors called out their wares. 'Milko!' 'Old rags!' 'Coal!' 'Baker!' Travelling from door to door they made their deliveries. All on horse and cart with householders racing out of doors when they had departed to collect valuable manure heaped on the streets. These were the last remaining visible sights of an almost vanished Victorian age.

Outside the Boleyn public house from which seeped a pungent odour of hops we halted, breathless from passing the football to each other.

'What time is it?' Looking over at Gobel's cooked meat and sausage shop, we saw the gold letters on their outside clock. It was nearing twelve thirty.

'What are we doing then?' Georgie asked. 'The usual?' The usual was to wait until men queued at the turnstiles for tickets to enter the football grounds and then crawl on hands and knees under their usually reluctant legs into the grounds beyond.

By now, Lenny, Abo and Tucker had joined us, beckoning for us to follow them, running along Green Street and into a gap in the high wire fence which circled Boleyn Castle and then, when inside, along a path until we reached locked huge black gates, with injurious looking spikes on top of them.

Looking at Georgie and Jocky, I awaited their response to this unexpected change of tactics and watched them cast doubtful glances at each other and return the way we had come. Lenny and Tucker obediently stood close to Abercrombie pushing him upwards enabling him to grasp hold of one of the spikes and haul himself up and on top of the gates.

'Chuck the ball over,' he called out once he was over the other side. We followed him, painstakingly balancing our feet between the spikes before dropping to the ground and racing down another path that led to the lofty outer stone walls of Boleyn Castle. With energetic agility Abercrombie bounded up to the wall, soon finding a foothold half-way up its face and, with Tucker close behind him, hauled himself over it and down to the other side. Struggling behind, Lenny and I, lacking the equanimity of the other two, eventually managed to climb up beside them.

Our next task was to jump down to where directly below a long rusty corrugated shed leaned against the wall where inside men would stand relieving themselves while standing in pools of a mixture of once white disinfectant and increasing amounts of urine. As we boys landed with reverberating thuds upon the roof shed, out scurried men suddenly interrupted from their intimate function, yelling at us and brandishing their fists while threatening us coarsely with what they would do to us if they caught up with us! Taking advantage of how we had surprised the men, nimbly we boys dropped to the ground and scooted away from their wresting attempts to deal with us.

Gasping for breath but grinning confidently at our achievement, we all then scurried like rabbits along the dark underground tunnels that led to where the football stands lay waiting for the crowds to fill them.

'Oi! You boys! Where're you going?' At the end of the tunnel standing clearly outlined by the light behind them, stood two stewards whose job it was to marshal the crowds along the tunnels and to keep out young interlopers like us. As they started to walk towards us we turned around speedily retracing the way we had arrived only to be confronted by other stewards equally as vigilant looking as those behind us.

'Run for it!' One of us called out and dashing headlong around the men, avoiding their outstretched arms, within seconds found ourselves back at the castle's stone wall. Once again Abercrombie with self-assured dexterity was the first of us to scale the wall and looking down at Tucker called out to him.

'Chuck us the ball Tuck!' Hesitating before he and Lenny and I managed to try and haul each other to the top of the wall. Tucker threw him the ball with experienced accuracy. Endeavouring to catch the ball with one hand. Abercrombie lost control of his firm footing and after reeling backwards and then forwards, finally started to fall down to earth. Then as he plummeted half-way down, a thudding sound startled us into watching him dangle suspended, as if on a gibbet, gulping and gasping for breath, hooked up by his scarf which had become entangled onto one of the spikes on the top of the wall.

Behind us had now gathered some of the crowds of spectators entering the grounds for the coming match and at the front of them the stewards who with immediate appreciation of the hazardous situation formed a base at the foot of the wall with their backs acting as a springboard enabling one of them to leap upwards and disentangle the scarf from the spike and for another to cradle Abercrombie's body into his arms and lift him downwards.

'Don't touch him!' A uniformed man in black and white was kneeling beside Abercrombie's collapsed body.

'It's the St John's Ambulance man,' someone muttered assuringly.

Cowed, frightened looks passed between Lenny and me, questioning Abercrombie's unfortunate plight. Would he survive? Very soon an ambulance arrived and he was speedily taken away. Lifeless. Or so it seemed to us.

Slowly the crowd moved away now bent on finding their way to the stadium stands and watch the forthcoming afternoon's match.

Some weeks later, squatted on the school hall's floor, nursing our stinging hands, Lenny, Geogie, Tucker and I, recovering from 'six of the best', listened, chastened, to old Cookie, our headmaster angrily lecture all of us on the foolhardiness of such an escapade, which would not be tolerated and to be grateful that the police had decided not to take any further action! Standing on a platform glaring down at us, he resembled an outraged orang-utan with silver-rimmed spectacles glinting threateningly in the semi-darkness.

All eyes strayed over to where Abercrombie sat with his neck encased in a plaster cast and a half-smile of smug contentment on his face.

It was some time before Lenny and I ventured into that football stadium again. Instead we reluctantly decided it would be more prudent to attend the Saturday afternoon show at the Boleyn cinema, where forced to listen to an organ recording of Bach's Toccata and Fugue blasting our ears from where we sat in the cheapest seats at the far side of the cinema before the first picture started was a price to pay and a safer bet.

But that's another story.

HOW ARE THE MIGHTY FALLEN
Liz Richards

Birdy Partridge had lived in great contentment at number seven, Hawthorne Drive throughout his married life. Great contentment, that is, until Alf Freeman moved into number nine. It had been downhill all the way after that.

Birdy's mother despaired of his nickname. She had agonised long and hard in The Sunshine Lying-In Home until she decided to call him George after her dear King. And within two years, all her pretensions to royal affiliation had come to nothing. For Birdy he had become and Birdy he was to remain. This was in some part due to a certain resemblance to his eponymous feathered counterpart, for even as a very young lad he had been full-bellied, with a curious, slightly strutting gait. But there the resemblance ended. Instead of wary hooded avian eyes, his own danced and glowed like embers in a draught.

He did well at school and obtained a good job in the shipping office. He met, courted and married Marjorie and they moved into number seven after their honeymoon in Teignmouth. There was a fair bit to do since a doodlebug had landed in the garden of number three in 1942, causing multiple cracks in the plaster and some misalignment of window and door frames, but Birdy was a whiz with his hands and immediately set about radical repairs. Once the house was in order he moved on to the garden and demolished the air raid shelter that bestrode the entire boundary between his and the next-door garden. The shelter was huge, must have been meant for the entire drive.

In due course, Claire and William arrived. Birdy was a strict but fair father who only wanted the best for his children. He played tennis with them at the rec, took them swimming and was instrumental in building the sets for the Scout pantomime each Christmas. As the children grew older he became active in Round Table and naturally, because of his innate rotundity and sparkling eyes, it was always he who donned the Santa outfit and toured Acacia, Cedar and Hawthorne Drives to raise money for those less fortunate than himself. Birdy was a brick.

The children grew up and moved. There were many empty-nesters in Hawthorne Drive. Bill and Monica Foster, next door, decided to sell up and decamp to Benidorm because of Monica's arthritis; a move they were to regret with the advent of mass tourism a decade later.

So that is how, on a balmy September evening, Birdy introduced himself to Alf Freeman over the garden fence. Alf clutched a bottle of stout in one hand and gestured expansively with the other.
'Nice enough area,' he volunteered.
'Too true,' responded Birdy enthusiastically. 'We all get on like a house on fire. Got a street party planned for the Queen's Silver Jubilee, you know. I'm Committee Chairman; why don't *you* join us? The more the merrier!'
Alf, scratching himself absently through the string vest which was his only upper garment, appeared indifferent to this idea. He leaned confidentially towards Birdy and hissed, 'Got any blacks living round here then?'
Birdy, taken aback, considered the question.
'Well, there's Doctor Wickramsingh at number thirty. And Mrs Williams in Cedar, she's a midwife. Nice families.'
Alf spat explosively and copiously on the ground.
'Hate the bastards,' he said.

'I hope I'm wrong,' said Birdy to Marjorie as they sipped their bedtime Ovaltine, 'but I suspect the Freemans may not be quite *our* sort of people. Guess what he -'
His remaining words were drowned out by the sound of a high-powered drill apparently intent on bursting through the party wall. Birdy glanced at the frantically shimmying wall clock and nodded meaningfully at Marjorie. Eleven-ten.
Instead of the reassuring swoosh of the teasmade, Birdy was woken next morning by a fusillade of lump hammer blows. He peered at his watch. Five-thirty! Were these the neighbours from hell?

Two years later and things were quietening down. Alf appeared to have finished eviscerating his home; his motorbike was now back on the road after much high-rev engine testing. Even the domestic friction chez Freeman had abated. True, the screaming and smashing of crockery had been superseded by a series of raucous parties, presumably of a celebratory nature, but even these were fewer now. To Birdy's relief Alf turned to the much more acceptable hobby of gardening.

Alf was planting a hedge. Digging was not one of his favourite occupations but he was sick to his guts of that bloody nosy Partridge bloke. Peering over, offering to show him how to tune the bike, help to move the pile of rubble, assist in installing the 'Acros'. He swigged from his beer bottle and picked up yet another leylandii.

They appeared above the fence, delicate green fronds waving in the breeze, a year later. Twelve months on and they were eight feet high. By the time they reached thirty feet only a thin pencil line of sunlight penetrated Birdy's garden and that for barely half an hour at high noon.
Summer bedding plants went first. Then the roses, the honeysuckle and the clematis. The lawn began to die.
'Sorry mate, no can do,' was Alf's response to Birdy's entreaties. 'On my land you see. Englishman's home is his castle and all that!'
Unable to spend his evenings in the garden, Birdy took to going down to the Pig and Whistle.

The general opinion in the snug was that there was little that could be done. The trees were on Alf's land so could not be touched. Clandestine poisoning was mooted but no one seemed to know what product would do the trick. Someone suggested ringing the bark, but this idea was abandoned as no one was willing to risk trespassing on Alf Freeman's land, not with his temper and a rumour that he had a gun.

Despondently, Birdy went to the bar to order another pint.

The man was new to the Pig and Whistle. His weather-beaten face, dark hair and silver earring proclaimed Romany origins.
'Are you new round here, then?' Birdy asked. He proffered his hand. 'Birdy Partridge's the name. Can I get you one in?'
'That's kind of you. I've got a bit of a thirst on - been hard at it at Hawshaw House all afternoon. Amias Smith, by the way.'
Birdy pocketed his change and raised his glass in salute.
'So what brings you to these parts?' he asked.

Birdy listened incredulously. He had never realised that moles could be such a problem. Had rather always thought of them as the avuncular Moley of long-ago pantomimes. Gentlemen in velvet overcoats.

'No way,' explained Amias. 'Nasty little sods. Claws that could rip your arm open from elbow to wrist. Patrol their tunnels twice a day searching for worms, almost blind but a fantastic sense of smell. Traps rarely work. Gas does, but you kill one off and two more move in and take over.

Breeding season's soon so they're expanding their territory. The damage they do, it's unbelievable. Gardens can cave in. They've brought whole trees down at Hawshaw House.'

'So how *do* you get shut of them?' asked Birdy.

Amias tapped the side of his nose conspiratorially.

'You send for me,' he said. 'I'm a mole charmer. I entice them out and . . .'

He brought the side of his hand down hard on the bar.

'Finito.'

A germ of an idea blossomed in Birdy's brain.

'Sure,' said Amias. 'I don't *have* to kill them. I *could* let them loose in that fellow's garden. But sod's law, they'd probably invade *you* instead.'

'Well, actually, no,' replied Birdy happily. You see, he planted them on the site of an old air raid shelter. Demolished it myself but I could never manage to get the footings out, they went down twelve feet. Withstood the Luftwaffe. What's a few moles?

A month later, Birdy peeped over the fence and calculated. The molehill count was up to over two hundred. He noticed with satisfaction that a couple of the leylandii were beginning to tilt towards Alf's garden.

As you know, Birdy was a brick. He was not a vindictive man. He knocked on Alf Freeman's door to warn him that part of his hedge was looking rather dickey and perhaps, just perhaps, he would be wise to move his Harley Davidson.

MISSION IMPOSSIBLE
Emma Jane Stroud

There are various ways that social mobility and the envy of others can be achieved, marriage being the most obvious route, education another, but attending midnight mass was one of the more unusual. 'Come on Jocasta, we'll be late,' Jean called up the stairs, it was 10.30pm on Christmas Eve and Jean wanted a good seat near the front amongst the well-bred, well away from the general 'riffraff'. As they went off up the road, the car spluttered and back-fired. 'Why don't you change this for something smaller and more reliable' Jocasta said emphasising the word 'reliable'. Jean fell silent, when would her only child understand a car's age and reliability was immaterial, it was its make that mattered and this was a Volvo and therefore had cache. As they 'kangerooed' into the church car park, Jean, agitated by the presence of others that may have seen their clown car-like entrance, fiddled with the knot on her royal standard design head scarf. Jocasta smiled as she watched her mother. Jean had once heard a neighbour say to another that she looked like the Queen when wearing it, as a royalist, Jean took this as the supreme compliment, from that day on Jean always wore her head scarf, not even the heatwave of 1977 deterred her.

'Good Evening Vicar,' said Jean in a loud voice so she caught everyone's attention, inwardly praising the church's acoustics, she continued, 'you remember my daughter, Jocasta, she is a curator at the Fitzwilliam Museum in Cambridge where she lives and studied, remember I bought her PhD research paper and graduation photographs around to show you? Jocasta flushed with embarrassment said hello and added the correction that she was an assistant curator. The vicar gave her a sympathetic and understanding smile. Whilst Jean attended his services every week he was reluctant to describe her as a Christian.

Jean was like a butterfly always looking out for a bigger and brighter flower. The end result was that she didn't have a single friend, leaving a great deal of time to think about Jocasta and what she wanted her to achieve at work and in society, Jean was thrilled that everything was going so well.

The family AGM, as Jean liked to call it, was always held over Christmas Day lunch. Jean presided; in fact Jean did all the talking.

After so many years in the chair she took agreement for granted. As in previous years, Jean would outline all she 'hoped' Jocasta would achieve over the next twelve months. The inflection Jean put on the word 'hope' demanded total compliance, and until now she had met with little resistance. There had admittedly been a slight hiccup fifteen years ago, when Jocasta's father or 'The Free Spirit' as Jean scornfully called him had left. Unable to cope anymore with the targets he too, had to achieve at work and in the community. Jean told people (those she harangued in changing rooms and newcomers to church and Mothers' Union) that she was, in fact, a widow (it was more middle-class), and despite all the economic hardship she had to endure, her daughter had achieved a doctorate from Cambridge. Jean not unwittingly played the role of the martyr to perfection. Then she would pause in her repartee and wait for them to say she must be very proud. It was by now a very polished performance, which had only increased in length over the years as Jocasta's academic achievements grew: 8 GCSEs at Grade 'A', 3 'A' Levels at Grade 'A', a First Class Honours degree and finally a Doctorate.

As they helped themselves to turkey, Jean began phase two of her bombardment; how long did Jocasta think it would be before she was made a curator? Was there anyone about to retire or seriously ill? And the thousand times-asked question, was she making it clear to management that she wanted to get on within the museum? After all, she had a PhD, Jean saw this as her talisman, and Jocasta felt it was a noose held by her mother around her neck, she tried to interject and was rebuffed.

According to Jean, she was to concentrate solely on her career, if she must marry then she should put it off until after the menopause, there would be no chance of children putting her off Jean's career path. But then if she did feel maternal, why not then look for a divorcee? She could become like a favoured aunt to her stepchildren without any of the inconveniences a natural mother had to bear. This had brought pity into the range of emotions Jocasta felt for her mother.

Rising from the table after pudding, Jean raised 'Any Other Business' and in the same breath moved to bring the meeting to a close, Jocasta cut her off mid-sentence. 'Yes' growled Jocasta more sternly than she had intended, taken aback Jean dropped back down into her seat. Jocasta firmly told Jean she would have to miss the Queen's Speech as she had twenty-five years of any other business to get through. That the plans as unveiled at today's AGM were totally unacceptable.

Jocasta began, her thin-lipped audience for once silent and possibly listening. Firstly, Jocasta stated that she would never become a curator, because she had handed in her notice in October and was now technically employed. Like the true professional pushy mother, with selective hearing, that she was, Jean soon recovered from this revelation and focusing on the word 'technically' asked when Jocasta was starting at the Victoria and Albert Museum in Kensington. According to 'The Plan' Jocasta wasn't due to start work there for five years. All too aware of this, Jocasta didn't answer and moved onto item two on her agenda. Whilst recovering from flu in the early autumn, Jocasta said she had suddenly realised this was the first break she had *ever* had from work or study, and had taken the opportunity not only to relax but to evaluate her life so far using her skills as a historian. She hadn't liked her conclusions. All she saw was study and Jean; setting targets that she had unwittingly achieved without question all her life, so far. The present saw an unhappy and very tired young woman with nearly, but not quite, as few friends as her mother.

Steeling herself Jocasta raised item three. That whilst off work, she had been visited by a colleague and they had found they had a great deal in common, friendship had quickly blossomed into love and they were to be married. At this point Jean started to cry, her dreams shattering. Jocasta, where she once would have abandoned her true dreams, pressed on relentlessly, she told her mother how kind and considerate he was and how, most importantly to her, he allowed her to voice her opinions and whilst not always agreeing with them, did acknowledge their validity. Only 'unemployed' and 'marriage' now rang in Jean's ears, suddenly she was jolted back into the room . . . 'He's called Imran,'

Jocasta explained, 'not a practising Muslim' she added, aware of the prejudicial stereotypes racing across Jean's mind.

Abruptly Jean rose from the table and again in a curt voice said she had a lot to think about and would say goodnight, it was only 6.30pm. Retiring to her room when not immediately getting what she wanted was standard practice. Thankfully Jocasta thought the charade of her mother packing or telephoning the orphanage was no longer a credible ploy. Once the bedroom door closed Jocasta rang Imran.

The next morning Jocasta made breakfast, when her mother finally came down, another psychological tactic; she was holding two unsealed envelopes, one addressed, the other not, and she put them both on Jocasta's side plate. Jocasta had prepared herself for 'Poor Me', another role her mother had perfected, to skulk into the room but the triumphant figure before her was new and she was unsure how to react. Looking down at her side plate she saw that the addressed envelope was to the Head of Personnel, at the Fitzwilliam. Jocasta opened the envelope. The typed letter inside said that she had had time to reconsider her resignation and realising what a waste of her PhD the decisions she had made regarding her personal life were, could she be reinstated in her old position as from January? The other envelope contained a letter to Imran terminating their engagement.

'If you'll just sign both letters and put his address on the envelope' Jean said in her now-resumed and familiar authoritarian tone . . .
Rising from the table Jocasta went upstairs.

When the front door slammed shut a short while later, Jean was brought back to the present from her considerations of Jocasta's glorious future. She would obviously have to move to Cambridge to live with Jocasta. After all if she were such a terrible mother, Jocasta would spend more time at work and therefore would be promoted more quickly. Smiling, Jean thought how one day Jocasta would thank her, as she would for her Christian name too. Realising it was taking Jocasta a long time to post the letters Jean went out into the hall, she was stopped in her tracks by the sight of the two letters she had typed, torn to shreds on the hall table and another envelope propped addressed, 'Mum'. Jean opened it.

Dear Mum,

For many years I have tried to be the daughter you wanted, to my own detriment. Thankfully (not too late) I have realised that all that matters in life is to be happy and content, with you as my role model of the reverse, I know what to avoid. Although I do acknowledge the sacrifices you have made for me, your mission in life, it seems, is to make others envy what I have achieved and for yourself to bathe in the reflected praise, I have never had the time. However, I'm sure others, but not you, ask the question, at what price? Whilst in a misguided way I believe you do love me, it is never going to be possible for me to achieve enough to make you content. So I decline to accept your 'Mission Impossible' any longer.

I will send you our address in Pakistan and a photograph of our baby, yes; I'm pregnant and thrilled.

Jocasta.

THE PRIEST KING
Bridget Trafford

Jack touched her shoulder,

'Still thinking about our amazing find? Incredible . . . disturbing though; we were discussing it when you wandered off.'

A mild reproof, Claire did not respond.
She was at the edge of the Acropolis, gazing down at the bay. The huge orange round of the sun was sliding into the limitless depths of the ocean, the passive splendour, a strange contrast to the turmoil of her mind.
Backtracking over the day's events, trying to divert herself with data, Claire found concentration elusive. Instead, her mind flew like a bird to the painted image behind her eyes, an image which captured her like a rabbit in headlights.
After days of fruitless, painstaking toil, it had emerged, suddenly; one minute, just the fragmentary outline of a delicate limb, the next, in its entirety; an apparition . . . The Priest King.
Thus she silently named him, knowing he was not, from remembered frescoes of ancient Crete. The small group of amateur archaeologists stood back and gazed at the fruits of their labour. They exclaimed over the perfection of his form, the strength of colour in his faded majesty, the delicate, autocratic poise; they chattered his origins and originators, how they should preserve and then remove him; what authorities they should contact; what press it would attract. And all the while she and he had stood in silent communication, soul to soul, down the aeons that separated them. And as she watched it seemed as if the great grey eyes turned toward her and one of the long, tapering hands had lifted in salutation. And Jack continued.

'Doesn't fit with what we know of the period. Certainly doesn't match in with the pottery we've found.'
'Couldn't he have just been a visitor?'
'For Christ's sake, Claire, engage the brain! He's a wall painting, not a bloody fossil!'
'Yes, of course.'
'Are you OK?'
'Yes, of course.'

'Claire!'
'I'm just tired.'
'Is that an invitation?'

Christ. Men!
She smiled. The past receded; the sunset was beautiful, the breeze warm, and they were standing amidst the ruins of an ancient, abandoned city . . .

'If you like.'

She did not remember leaving the curtains open. White light, powerful as the beam of a headlight, was forcing through her eyelids, flooding her mind with images. One image; she opened her eyes, her mind clear and focused and turned to look at Jack. His face was calm, untroubled by dreams, and she felt a pang of remorse, but could not have said why. She dressed and let herself out of the room, ran lightly down the stairs and out into a night lit by a thousand torches. On an escalator of moonlight she ran, then walked and finally climbed through bleached bone rocks, back to the Acropolis of Amathus. As she reached the top, the moon's brilliance, and the clarity of her mind combined in a vortex, which focused on the ancient temple walls.
The colours of his elegant pleated skirts sang with brilliance, the soft folds of blue, the blue of Grecian skies and church domes, was echoed in the intricate woven headdress, with its elegant plumes. The perfectly-formed limbs were long, lean and supple, touched with the sun of the gods, aloof, regal, but with a devastatingly tangible beauty. Perhaps it was a trick of the moonlight or the pounding in her head that was making the colours deepen, the outlines become more firm. But it was the eyes, drawing her in and down, as if by letting go she would fall . . . fall . . .

The day was hot. Claire sat on the periphery of the group, mechanically polishing a fragment of pottery, her fingers moving with rhythmic calm, while her thoughts chased each other, round and round like hamsters in a cage. Watching, she recoiled with horror each time a practised

archaeological hand traced the fine lines of his body, and scholastic eyes probed his crazed limbs. Cautious minds shared theories of time and place. When one of the group took up a small knife to scrape away some of the surface plaster from his lower leg, Claire felt the touch of the blade as if against her own flesh, and cried out in pain.
Jack came hurrying over, his face all consternation.

'What's wrong, for God's sake?'

She recovered herself quickly, pulling back at the sound of his voice. It left her with a sensation of being outside, as if material and spirit world had manifested, in parallel, and she, a bystander, part of neither.

'It's OK.' The voice came from beyond. More emphasis. 'Really!' Desperately. 'Look, I'm fine. Just hot. And I think something bit me.'

She squinted up at him, his face a mask of paternal concern and doubt, and irritation rose like a flood, banishing the last vestiges of unreality.

'Stop looking at me like that! I've said I'm OK, haven't I? Just leave it will you!'

He turned away, but not before she saw the hurt. Remorse tightened her throat and made her reach out a hand, but there was no chance.

'Let's call it a day, guys. I vote we go take a shower and all meet up at Plato's in about an hour.'

It was not a suggestion and no one argued.

'I'm going for a walk.' Claire was conscious of a dozen pairs of eyes swivelling between them. 'I'll catch you later.'

She stood abruptly and then turned to glance back, past Jack, with his commandeering gaze, past the curious bystanders, to the regal stranger in his rocky domain. But his stance was remote and his gaze unfocussed and she felt curiously bereft . . .

She started off down the hillside with no further intention than to put distance between herself and the site. After five minutes she found her feet following an ancient track, overgrown but quite distinct. It led unerringly from the Acropolis down to the shore, where, now separated from the site by a road, the ruined harbour of Amathus lay, almost entirely submerged. Away from the claustrophobia of the dig, the air was cooler, and the sense of purpose which had driven her from her bed the previous night, invaded her again.

Reaching the road she turned back towards the town where they were staying. Stopping at the first taverna, with its usual profusion of souvenirs and provisions, she bought a snorkel and mask.

It was an underwater world of magic, history reshaped and preserved, spangled with colour from showers of tiny fish, dispersing at her approach and reforming in her wake. She swam lazily, allowing the water to cool and restore. In a rocky cleft, still blue among the slivers of movement, the necklace lay. She recognised it before her mind made the connection. A triple strand, the centre one made up of tiny gold lilies, interspersed with beads of lapis lazuli, the two outer of pure lapis, their penetrating colour reflecting the azure blue of his headdress, with its wonderful plumes.

The site was deserted when she returned. The sun was dropping in the sky, gilding the whole hillside into a gift for kings.

His colours were stronger too. The lines of his fine limbs, his strong profile, the wonderful plumed headdress, all defined by unseen hand. His wrists and ankles were adorned with intricately worked ornamentation, but his throat was bare. The necklace lay in the palm of her hand, its fine strands hanging through her fingers. She moved toward him, stooped and laid it at the foot of the wall. When she raised her head, the magnificent dark eyes were looking straight into hers.

Claire was first on site the next day. She had told no one of her find and she felt strangely conspiratorial as she stood before the fresco. The necklace had gone. His colours were pale with time, but around his neck was a magnificent triple stranded collar of lapis lazuli and gold. Someone touched her shoulder and she braced herself.

'Interesting.'

He'd noticed! Fool! How could he miss it? She realised she was holding her breath.

'Found something interesting in the local archives yesterday . . . while you were lazing in the sun . . .'

Her easy lie came back at her like a dart, but she didn't react and he passed on.

'There was an archaeological team here in 1930 The museum has some sketchy details of their finds. Apparently they found evidence of a Minoan fleet which briefly touched these shores in around 1800BC. Picked up quite a few finds in the harbour area. Several of them are believed to have been destroyed. The project was shelved for some reason . . . probably lack of funds . . .'

So that was how he came to be so far from home! A storm perhaps; or maybe sabotage . . . No matter . . . it had happened and he had been stranded here, in a foreign land, an outcast with no means of escape, until now . . .
Jack was still talking. But in her moment of clarity, Claire was alone. She had only to wait . . .

She passed the day in a state of untroubled equilibrium. The discussion ebbed and flowed. Plans were made to go to a taverna, popular for its live music, and she agreed indifferently. Jack's relief was so tangible, she wanted to laugh, but could feel no guilt . . .

This time she did not sleep. Behind her closed eyes Minoan long ships tossed helplessly on high seas. She lay quite still, until the moon's light dispersed the pictures and filled her mind with diamond clarity. Then she rose, dressed and without haste, made her way to the harbour. For a few moments she stood looking down through the silvered depths to the shadowed walls beneath. A shallow breeze stirred the hair at the back of her neck and a shiver ran up her spine. It seemed to gain in intensity and the bent cypress at the water's edge murmured in response, and she heard her name. Soft at first, no more than a whisper; then more insistent.

Without hesitation she crossed the empty road and unfalteringly stepped onto the ancient road which led to the Acropolis. It was some moments before she realised that the path was no longer overgrown. Like a ribbon of woven light, it led directly to the temple walls. Strangely calm, she began the ascent. As she climbed, she noticed a new order in the ruins, as if an unknown hand had tossed them all up in the air and they had fallen back in their original symmetry. Reaching the summit, she paused, lost for a moment in wonder and awe. The temple facade was restored to its original glory, and stood bathed in light, set against the ink-blue of the night sky. Looking back down the hillside she saw the path, obscured by darkness and strewn with fragments of stone, shards of pottery and tangled undergrowth.

She entered the temple through the gate. Its walls were smooth, painted with intricate patterns in deep blue, soft brown and cream. But the wall painting had gone . . .

'Claire!'

The sound was clear and light. She turned her head . . .

Jack Thurnham awoke alone. Driven by a sense of urgency he did not understand, he went straight to the site. In the clear morning light everything was as he remembered. Everything, that is, except the fresco. The wall was empty. Just a rough-hewn surface with some ancient plaster fragments clinging to its surface. There was no sign of Claire. His eye caught a glimmer of something at the base of the wall. He moved across to it, stooped, picked it up. In the palm of his hand, the three-stranded collar of lapis lazuli and gold winked back at him in the strengthening morning light.

THE SIXTH EXTINCTION

A LETTER TO THE FUTURE
(To whom it may concern)
Tony Webster

I do not know what shape or form you have (or even if you have form, as we know it), or even when in the future you will be reading this letter (if 'reading' is not too loose a term), but if someone *is* reading it, at some distant future time, please persevere, hear my story - and don't judge us *too* harshly.

I have no doubt, whatsoever, that what 'you' (I will call you that because even a body without form must have sentience and self) find here on this earth will be bleak barren desolation, utterly devoid of life, the only proof that life had once existed here being these brief, hurried, inadequate letters, buried deep in the hope of being found one day. We have deposited them, individually and collectively, (together with a full visual archive of our mores and times - 'O tempora, O, mores!' - in which is contained the whole range and gamut of human experience, philosophy, emotion, history and culture), in a variety of forms, hoping that our beacon will be seen or heard and at least one of these will be decipherable and understandable to future visitors visiting our Earth, either by design or by chance encounter - explorers, probably - invaders, conquerors, probably not. For one thing, you will find nothing left to conquer and secondly, I firmly believe that 'people' capable of travelling between the stars, will have evolved beyond the petty bickering, warring and need to subjugate each other that has brought *us* to this sorry state.

Like you, we had aspirations of space travel. We journeyed the small distances to our moon and to our nearest planets and thought we were Gods by so doing.

> 'My name is Ozymandias, King of Kings:
> Look on my works, ye Mighty and despair!'

The whole complex history of man, with its dreams, culture, history and art, great literature, thousands of years of exploration, space travel, all his achievements past, present and to come, is now no more.

We had it all, we thought. Great literature, poetry, music, architecture, art.

The literature of Chaucer, Shakespeare and Homer, of Molière, Jane Austen and A A Milne, J K Rowling, and George Bernard Shaw.

> 'To die: to sleep;
> To sleep; perchance to dream: ay, there's the rub;
> For in that sleep of death what dreams may come?
> When we have shuffled off this mortal coil,
> Must give us pause.'

The music of Beethoven, Mozart, Chopin, and Brahms, of Charlie Parker, Gershwin, Elvis Presley, and John Lennon - the plaintive strains of the second movement of the Bruch Violin Concerto in G Minor, the energy and dynamism of a Buddy Holly song, the relentless, restless rhythms of 'Rhapsody in Blue', the foot-tapping resonance of ragtime by Scott Joplin or the magic and mystery of a Beatles' pop masterpiece - each equally worthy and fulfilling in its own way.

The poetry of Spenser, Christina Rossetti, Yeats and Keats, Dylan Thomas, Rupert Brooke, Sylvia Plath and Philip Larkin.

> 'O, what can ail thee, knight at arms?
> Alone and palely loitering?
> The sedge has withered from the lake,
> And no birds sing.'

From Beowulf and Gawain to Archie Rice and Sebastian Flyte (and Aloysius the bear).

The art and creativity (and genius) of Leonardo da Vinci, Michelangelo, Constable and Turner, Andy Warhol, David Hockney, Pollack and Picasso, none of whom prosecuted their art for profit or fame, but for some deep inner satisfaction and sense of achievement - for its own sake.

Great architects of man's finest structures - Wren, Gilbert Scott, Le Corbusier and Frank Lloyd Wright - palaces and monuments, stadiums and cathedrals, but also homes and schools, churches and shopping centres. Inventors, scientists, and innovators from Leonardo (again) to

Albert Einstein, from Stephen Hawking to Trevor Baylis, John Logie Baird and Tim Berners-Lee.

Entertainers, too - the dancers, jugglers, magicians, comedians down the ages, who make and have made us laugh - made us forget our problems, and our trials and tribulations, for a short while. The film makers, the photographers, the illustrators, the cartoon industries - from 'Mickey Mouse' and 'Snow White' to 'The Lion King' and 'The Flintstones', from 'Gone With the Wind' and 'The Third Man' to 'Educating Rita' and 'Star Wars'. We admired and made icons of our celluloid heroes - Marilyn Monroe, Robert Redford, Cliff Richard, Geena Davis - wanted to be like them - to live their lives.

But we were also, millions of us, very ordinary, unpretentious, decent, kindly people. We loved beauty and nature, created and cultivated and nurtured our gardens, admired creativity in every form, loved, and were loved - made love! A few of us aspired to greatness or had greatness thrust upon us and achieved it or triumphed over some handicap or adversity, becoming famous or infamous, depending on society's viewpoint or conventions, others tried and failed and, by so doing, demonstrating their very humanity in that failure. Most of us, though, found what contentment and fulfilment we needed in the very ordinariness of our daily lives and, in our sublime innocence, wanted nothing more.

But we also always had the evils of strife and war, of dictators and despots like Hitler and Stalin and Sadam Hussein, but also of the many great statesmen and women who opposed them - Churchill, Margaret Thatcher, Ghandi, and others. We should have learnt from this but we didn't. Each new nation coming to adulthood and independence wanted more and more power, possessions, wanted what the other nations had - technology, guns, weapons of war, with which to impose their will on others.

We had our dreams - over which we had little or no control. We made our nightmares, too - over which we found we had *no* control and which in the end controlled us.

And in the end we destroyed it all - pollution, greed, envy, ignorance, war. Pollution was just one factor. We burnt and used up all our fossil fuels, poisoned our atmosphere with 'greenhouse' emissions, destroyed the ozone layer with CFCs, released great clouds of radioactivity over the Earth and, in the process, killed millions of people. We abused the land, tore it apart, meddled with nature until it could no longer sustain us, created hybrids and gross mutations of crops and plants and of people.

Deforestation of huge tracts of land changed the climate, exterminated countless species of flora and fauna by eliminating their natural habitats. The 'knock-on' effects of this and other changes in their environment reverberated down the food chains world-wide sending species after species into extinction.

The 'small blue' butterfly, the green tree frog, the Indian tiger, the great mammals of the oceans, the whales, dolphins, and porpoises, all suffered. Once there were bison on the plains of North America as far as the eye could see - now there are only a few hundred.

Global warming melted the ice caps, raised sea levels, caused great tidal waves, floods, devastation, made life untenable in many parts.

We were envious of each other's property and land. We despised anything and anyone who was different from us, using them; subjugating and exterminating those we thought were lesser beings. Some of us, native peoples like the North American Indians, the Maoris and the Ancient Aborigines of the Southern Continents, were different, had respect for the land and for all living things, but they were not enough. They were despised, too, for their beliefs, and subjugated and their voices muted.

We fought each other for anything at all - for things, for mates, for property, for land, for 'ideals', both religious and cultural. This deadly weakness, this intolerance and contention, eventually and inevitably escalated into full-scale battles and wars. We developed new and more efficient instruments of war, from spears and swords, to guns and tanks, to battleships and bombs, to nuclear missiles and beyond, committing whole economies to this end - and in the end it destroyed *us*.

We learnt, but we learnt too late. We buried our grievances, settled our differences (because we had to), tried to mend the damage, renew the forests, to 'patch things up', but it was too late, things had gone too far.

Our world is dying; parts of it are already dead. How long it will be, we don't know.

> 'Do not go gentle into that good night,
> Rage, rage, against the dying of the light.'

As a last and fitting gesture to the ordinary people of Earth, who were so cruelly robbed of their heritage and birthright by the rulers and the shakers and makers - the politicians and the military, I exercise my last duty, as an ordinary citizen of the world, to pass on this personal (and unofficial) message, to whosoever it will concern, at such time as it is seen.

I am not, therefore, by definition, a great orator, diplomat, or speechmaker and cannot express myself as well as I would like, but maybe that is the best way. These few, inadequate words and brief references cannot possibly do justice to the whole of man's history and achievements, but maybe it is fitting that I do so.

In the belief that this has happened many times before, I urge you (perhaps as others have been urged before) to *learn* from our mistakes. If you are the seeding of a new Earth (as we may have been many aeons ago), start again on this old Earth. Make it rich and beautiful again. Create great literature, music, art, poetry, again. Love and be loved.

> 'It was the best of times, it was the worst of times.'

> It was our time . . .

Tony Webster

MEMORIES
Gwen Liddy

Anne had made a fool of herself and she knew it.

Sitting alone on the bench overlooking the bay her face still flushed with anger and embarrassment, she looked back at the hotel with its white walls contrasting against the dark green of the forest and wondered why she had let it happen like that. As her anger gradually subsided she realised she would have to return to the hotel, apologise to the hotel proprietress, Mrs Phillips, and, if he was still there, to the man who had been the cause of her furious outburst at the breakfast table. She would pack her bag and leave knowing that she could never return to the hotel that meant so much to her.

The 'Bay View Hotel' was where she and John had spent their honeymoon returning the following year to celebrate their first anniversary. In her emotive state she cried out aloud.

'Oh! John, John. Why did it have to happen to you? Why?'

Two years ago Anne had waved John off to work from the doorway of their bungalow near the East Sussex town of Wadhurst. They had that morning talked over their holiday plans to return to 'Bay View' for the third time. John always left his City office in time to catch the 17.22 train from Cannon Street to Wadhurst Station, then a short walk and he was home before seven o'clock.

When on that day, that awful day in March, John did not arrive at his usual time Anne at first was not worried. Trains from Cannon Street were often late and although he had his mobile he may not have been able to use it. At eight o'clock she did begin to worry. John should have been home or phoned by now.

Anne had only a hazy recollection of what happened next. She vaguely remembered seeing a policeman at the door and of him saying to her

'Mrs Palmer?' I'm afraid I have to tell you your husband was taken ill on Cannon Street Station, he was taken to hospital - I believe a heart attack - they did all they could but I'm sorry to have to say he died on the operating table. Is there anything we can do for you?'

Anne simply refused to accept it.

She kept everything of his, his books, slippers, pipe just where he had left them. He would always be with her, she would not, she could not, let him go. That is why, after the funeral, she had travelled alone to the little Devonshire hotel, 'Bay View', they called their holiday home, to spend a quiet time with her memories of John.

On the third day of her stay, Anne was at breakfast with the six elderly couples that made up the clientele when the quiet of the hotel was shattered by the roar of a sports car entering the forecourt. Through the window Anne saw the driver, a fair-haired man in his early thirties dressed casually in a checked sports jacket, jump out, grab a bag from the vacant passenger seat and stride purposefully into the foyer. She heard a loud voice enquiring about a room. She heard raucous laughter and Mary, the maid, giggling at something said. It was all in such contrast to the gentility of 'Bay View' and its guests that Anne felt strangely disturbed.

Mary brought the man into the dining room and showed him to a table. He was soon in loud, friendly, conversation with those around him. Several times he tried to catch Anne's eye but she always looked away. She hastily finished her meal and departed hoping this newcomer would not stay long.

At dinner that same evening the man, who had announced himself as Richard Wells, kept everyone, except Anne, amused with his cheerful banter. Mary in particular seemed taken by him. On leaving the room he stopped at Anne's table.
'Oh, Anne!' he said, you don't mind me calling you Anne, do you?'
Before Anne could concur or object, he went on, 'How would you like to come tomorrow for a drive in the old jalopy?'
Anne's reply was immediate, cool, but polite.
'No thank you, I am going somewhere.'
'OK.' He was not offended by her refusal. 'Another time.' He strode off.

Several times during the next few days Richard asked Anne if she would like a drive along the coast. Anne constantly refused; all she wanted was to be left alone with her memories of John and relive those happy days they had spent exploring the coast and countryside. She resented Richard's persistent approaches.

On the Friday morning, things came to a head. That day, had he lived, would have been John's thirtieth birthday and Anne had placed a birthday card by his photograph on the bedside table.

Dressed in a blue floral sun dress, white sandals and carrying a white matching handbag she went down to breakfast early, keen to make the most of John's special day.

Richard came in when she was halfway through her meal and came straight to her.

'Hello Anne,' he spoke almost eagerly, 'you're down early. You do look extra nice this morning. They say there is a fair on over at Tadworth Village, would you like to come? It will be fun, do say yes, you'll enjoy it, I'm sure.'

Anne was about to give her usual cool refusal when in a misguided effort to persuade her, he placed his hand on her bare shoulder.

That did it. Anne practically flew at him, no longer able to contain her anger.

She leapt to her feet, knocking over her glass of orange juice, spilling the juice over her dress.

'Why don't you leave me alone,' she virtually screamed at him, 'I don't want to go with you. Can't you understand? Go away. Stop pestering me.'

Richard jumped back as if he had been stung. The other guests stared in blank astonishment.

Anne, red-faced with embarrassment, pushed past him and fled the room. She ran from the hotel up the slope to the bench overlooking the bay.

She collapsed onto the seat, buried her face in her hands, and for the first time since John's death, wept uncontrollably. She felt for her handkerchief then realised she had left her bag behind.

She knew she had overreacted. She had made a fool of herself and she would have to go back and apologise. if only she had kept her cool, treated Richard with the same indifference she had shown before, this would not have happened. However, it had happened, there was now nothing for it but to go back, apologise, pack her bag and leave. She felt that she had spoilt John's birthday.

'Oh, John,' she cried aloud in her anguish, 'I'm so sorry.'

She was so engrossed in her thoughts she did not hear Richard approach.

'Anne.' She looked round, Richard stood hesitant, fearing another outburst. He was unsure how he should proceed, 'I thought you might want this.' He handed her her bag.

Anne was grateful to him at least for that.

'I'm sorry,' he said softly, his brash manner now gone he sounded genuinely contrite, 'I'm sorry if I said anything to upset you, that was the very last thing I wanted to do. I am really sorry.'

Anne, all her anger gone, shook her head.

'It wasn't your fault,' she said, 'I shouldn't have said what I did.'

'Mind if I sit down?' he said, still unsure.

Anne moved aside and he sat down. There was an awkward silence. Anne thought an explanation was needed. She spoke quietly. She told him everything, how she had waved her husband off to work on that fateful day two years ago and all that had happened since.

'To me,' she said with feeling, 'John is not dead. I feel his presence all the time, I know he is with me.'

To Richard, a stranger, maybe because he was a stranger, she was able to talk openly of her feelings.

'That is why 'Bay View' means so much to me.' She looked back at the hotel affectionately.

Richard had listened in silence then said gently, 'I know how you feel.'

Anne shook her head. 'Nobody,' she said, 'can know how I feel, what John meant to me.'

'A year ago,' Richard said, 'I was sent to Paris on a business trip. It was important I got a contract to make machine parts. The firm I worked for depended on it for without it the firm would go under. It was that vital.

The competition, especially from Germany, was strong but I did it. I phoned my boss to tell him the contract was signed and sealed. He was delighted and suggested I stay on in Paris, have a few days holiday at the firm's expense. I phoned my wife, Carol, we had a house near Epsom, and suggested she brought our two children, Janet and Robert, over for the weekend.

Carol and the kids were all excited. We had always promised them a trip to Disneyland and this seemed too good an opportunity to miss.

Carol had to move fast. She had to arrange for someone to look after the pets, book an evening flight from Gatwick, phone me, then drive to the airport in time to book in.

'I went to the airport and watched the flight land. They were not on it.
I phoned the reception at the hotel to see if Carol had left a message. There was a message but not from Carol. It was a message from the Embassy asking to see me urgently.

They told there had been an accident, it seems a lorry carrying inflammable liquid had jack-knifed in front of Carol's car. Carol was a good driver but she never had a chance, she stopped but a van ran into the back of them and shunted them into the pile-up. They were all - all killed.'

Richard's voice broke. Anne saw his face, so strong and manly, crumple like a child's she saw his hand resting on his knee tremble slightly. She instinctively covered his large hand with hers and pressed gently. There wasn't anything she could say.

After a moment or two, Richard recovered his composure, even managed a smile.
'So you see, Anne, I do know how you feel. I know it may sound hard but I thought the best way to come to terms with it was to try and wipe the tragedy from my mind. Forget it all. That is what I told myself Carol would have wanted.

I travelled around not stopping too long in any one place, making new friends, I wanted to forget I ever had a family. I wanted to but couldn't. I would see a girl with the same colour hair that Carol had, hear someone laugh the way she did, see children playing in the park. There were too many things that brought back too many painful memories for me ever to forget them. I tried all the harder to make new friends, in your case, Anne,' he smiled ruefully, 'I tried too hard.'
Anne managed a smile and a nod.
'I think,' Richard said, 'we have both tried different ways to come to terms with grief, neither of us has succeeded, have we?'

At that moment Anne felt John's presence stronger than ever before. She heard his voice clear inside her head.
'Time to let go Anne. Goodbye darling. Take care.'

Anne felt a weight lift from her shoulders. She turned to Richard, her eyes full of tears, her cheeks stained with mascara, but her smile was radiant.

'You asked me,' she said, 'if I would like to come to the fair with you, if the offer still stands, I would like to come. I really would.'

DREAM MAKER
Glenwyn Evans

I had never felt so utterly worthless and dejected. I'd like to kick the guy that said: 'You can achieve anything if you want too'! This had no meaning to me anymore. My inner strength and confidence had waned to an incredible all-time low.

This left me to contemplate one thing: In life you can only go as far as them that had power would let you.

Oh - how I hated people who lauded power over others.

I left the job centre without uttering a single word. The interview, to prove myself, was an utter flop. Still, I thought, I could always rely on my faithful best friend, Kirsten, she was always there for me . . .

I turned in the direction of The Crazy Coffee Shop only to see three youths gang upon some poor oriental lad.

'You've picked a bad day!' I growled, going in like fury, fists flying, feet kicking, until at last the scuffle was over and they ran off!

Imbrued with sweat and blood, I wiped my nose to speak to the youth, when almost at once he was dragged away unexpectedly by a number of mysterious looking officials.

'That was four months ago, Daniel, you have to get on with things,' Kirsten said assuringly, sipping her black coffee.
I shook my head grimly: 'There's something else I want to tell you,' I insisted, licking my lips. 'Since that day I've been getting the most weirdest dreams . . .'
'Dreams Daniel?' chuckled Kirsten quizzically as Gabrielle's 'Dreams can come true, baby' played in the background.
'Yeah, dreams I can't even remember,' I replied. 'All I know is every morning I wake up breaking cold sweat at the end of the dreams . . . Huh, whatever the dream was . . .'
'Was? But it is that yet destined to fall,' came a whispering voice.
Kirsten and I looked up over the tops of our coffee mugs where an old man of oriental persuasion stood aloft, flashing a cold grin.

'You dreamt . . . There was a queen ant and about her presence she had many, many other ants, all loyal, faithful to the last. But then, into her worldly palace entered a new ant. This ant was so different than any other they had ever yet come to know. For his bravery out-classed every other warrior ant. His shrewdness was above all other ants and his presence was most sort after, even by Her Royal Highness, herself. Then, you rose up to your full magnificence and all those insignificant ants that lay into your back, you shook off, treading them all into the dust and mire. Is that not the dream?'

'Yes - yes,' I stammered, incredulously.

'The interpretation is no longer obscure,' he whispered. 'Though you do not know it, you saved the life of an oriental princess travelling in disguise. It is she who is Queen. In one year's time you will be revered above all other subjects in our proud and ancient land, and you - yes you, Daniel Johnson, believe it or not; what you loath you will become - very powerful! As of the ants biting and rising upon your back, they will be disposed of, in time.'

Being a sceptic, I did not dwell on the matter, as a matter of fact, the whole thing carried a certain air of amusement for me, as well as Kirsten, until, one year exactly to that actual day, while nattering at The Crazy Coffee Shop, I was shangied by three impressive, oriental men posing as waiters, and shipped to a foreign land . . .

Everywhere I walked, soft petals were placed beneath my feet, and my robes, being of the finest quality, meant I walked amidst nobles.

It was all remarkable, too remarkable for I had picked up their beautiful, high pitched language, quite fluently and came to have many, many great debates and friends.

My martial arts peaked most adversaries that were thrown against me, and very soon, earned their great respect, winning many vicious, serious battles, some even to the death!

But then, one glorious, hot summer's day, while laying under the cool shade of a weeping willow, in this almost gothic-like ancient oriental place, I awoke to find I was being eaten alive! By ants!

Laughingly, I shook the tiny mites off my back when a great procession suddenly enrolled itself before me.

'Her Empress, the Great Lu Wann, awaits your presence.'
I could hardly believe it! Here, at last, was my chance to meet the lady,
(or should I say, lad, as I wrongly thought) whose life I'd saved.

To a wonderful fanfare, my eyes came to rest upon her, the Queen. The
most beautiful, oriental girl I had ever seen.

She stood erect; small, petite, yet elegant; eyes glimpsing that of stars
and moon while clothed in the robes of heaven's celestial sparkling
light; her hands, slightly tanned, long and thin, beckoned me to come
towards her.

And I, in all my innocence, I, who once looked scathingly upon those
who wielded power, greatness and authority; those who lauded it over
the weak; I, who hated all forms of law and order with utter disdain and
contempt, knelt, humbly before this, her most royal mantle.

My heart fluttered and so I fell under hypnotic spell, deeply, madly,
passionately, I was captivated, totally enthralled and forever lost in
love! I must win her, but how?

'Welcome,' said she, pleasantly, sweetly, as if singing to the tune of a
thousand vibrant harps. 'Loyal advisor to the Crown. For your
courageous acts, I make you the third most powerful being throughout
the land! Viceroy of Luan!'

After the passing of time, I learnt wisely on how to use my newly
acquired powers; it came about that great murders were being
committed throughout the land, and the Chief of Law, Le Lui, being the
second most powerful being in the land, was at a loss.

(I had also learned that it was only he that could marry the Empress!)

'What shall I do?' Le Lui cried one day, anxiously. 'Our land is scarred
with these vagabonds and thugs; pillaging villages, burning them to the
ground; taking towns' prefects, cutting their heads off and displaying
them on the end of pikes! The stench of blood of the innocents is falling
upon my head! My precious love will not like it!'
'It is anarchy of the worst kind,' I said, lowering the tone of my voice,
acknowledging his position with a courteous bow; observing for the

first time the golden ring of Anlu, upon his right hand, forth finger, sparkling brightly.

It was here, my countenance began to fall, for as he spoke, the more I coveted that ring; and the more I coveted that ring the more I knew I had to obtain it . . . The Queen . . . And with that, absolute power!
'The ring?' asked my loyal, treacherous friend, Chancellor Ming Wan. 'The ring, my friend, is a symbol of power that can only be removed by Her Majesty, Lui Wann. But,' paused he, prudishly, guessing my dishonest intentions, 'I do know for sure that once a month the diamonds, sapphires and rubies are removed to be cleaned, most regularly, for they must always be seen to gleam within the presence of Her Royal Highness.'

I pondered the situation thoughtfully, carefully and Ming Wan discerned my thoughts, very correctly.

'And,' he continued, his voice lowering as we walked along the hollow corridor, 'I have an idea on how you could obtain that very thing your heart desires, for it is written that only he that bares the ring of Anlu is allowed to marry our Crowned Empress . . .'
'Lui Wann,' I muttered, and an evil, wicked grin spread across my face.

'Why do you bring me here?' Le Lui quizzed angrily, bowing his head before her, the Great Empress, Lui Wann. 'Why do I find myself charged with high treason?' eyes levelling out suspiciously at the new Western Viceroy.
'I have proof, Le Lui, that you are the mastermind behind the anarchists. Do you deny this?' said I calmly.
Le Lui twitched nervously. I had him!
'What proof?' he stammered.
'Bring in the first witness,' I called with jubilant, masterful flourish.
'The jeweller?' whispered Le Lui, exchanging incredulous glances.
'I found two diamond stones missing from the Great Ring of Power your Most Honourable Majesty,' he announced, bowing lowly, then taking his place, respectively.

There came a rising groan, levelling off to astonished silence.

'And where were these two stones to be found?' I asked, eyes glaring back at Le Lui's cold, malignant stare. 'Bring in the second witness to the Crown, Chancellor Ming Wan!'

The prisoner, Le Lui, dropped back as if he had been stunned! Ming Wan took the stand before Her Majesty.
'I was approached,' said he in a calm, silvery voice. 'By an unusual vagabond with an extraordinary tale saying he had proof that the uprisings were brought about by no other than Le Lui!'
'Lies!' screamed Le Lui, shrieking hysterically. 'Why should I? I, who is betrothed to Her Most Loyal Majesty, Lui Wann,' he pleaded, tears glistening his cheeks.

Chancellor Ming Wann, unimpressed, delivered the fatal stroke to his master plan. 'I asked the vagabond his proof. He replied: 'What proof you need?' This is the proof he gives,' dropping two glittering diamonds to the floor with damning, dramatic effect.

The plebs roared! Her Majesty, Lui Wann, turned her back as also did all the other fine, dignified nobles.
'You are hereby condemned to death! By beheading!' I growled, satisfied with the outcome as he was dragged away, kicking, clawing; screaming obscenities, protesting his sincere innocence.

My Queen, Lui Wann, gave over the great ring of Anlu, and at once, I adorned my official robe, and put it on with a feeling of self-importance and great esteem.

And why not? Was I not in line to marry the most beautiful girl on earth? Now, nothing could stop me. For soon, I would become Emperor and then . . . Then my eye caught that sly, silvery smile of the Chancellor, Ming Wan!

Rule one: to bring someone down who knows more than he should, know his weaknesses! As it happened, I knew Ming Wan's most innermost weakness.

Opium!

Ming Wan, (whereas I never touch the stuff), just couldn't get enough of it, and that, sadly was his downfall. A self-inflicted overdose! 'Poor guy!' I cried. 'Poor, poor guy!'

One day, while attending Her Most Royal Majesty, two days before the wedding; while deliberating some of my western ideas for the new Luan, two thousand and one, I was approached by a most curious, if not awkward beguiled looking stranger.
'What do you want?' I questioned arrogantly.
'To tell you the meaning of your dreams,' spoke he, mildly.
'I don't have dreams,' I returned, clapping my hands, drawing the guards to the room.
'The ant! The unusual ant that stood up amongst all the others at the Royal Court. Remember?'
I swallowed my spit.
'I didn't tell you how the dream ends, did I not?'
'I know how the dream ends,' I replied, throat drying up quickly.
'Do you? Do you also know that the Great Ring of Power glows when it comes into contact with someone evil?'

The fourth finger on my right hand began to itch, the ring, to my utter amazement slipped off, clattering to the floor.
'Look! The Great Ring of Power, our Protector, is now beginning to protect Lui Wann from you, Daniel Johnson!'
I was seized almost immediately and dragged away . . .

My eyes awoke to a glaring sun. Above, hovering like an eagle, hung the silhouetted form of the executioner. Drums rolled, the man in black wielding a huge, silver object, danced and jigged. Then, flash!

Like a bolt, the old man shot up!

'No!' he cried nastily, shaking his head. 'A machine that can interact with life and mind? Never!' throwing the headset into the trash can . . .

'Ming Wan,' said Le Lui, picking up the phone. 'The Dream Maker, is now in my possession.'

OUR SISTER NE'ER DEPARTED
Peter S A Cooper

At first I remained at a little distance from all the others. I stood almost directly underneath the spreading boughs of one of the elms bordering the cemetery. I sensed something comforting in them after gazing at the endless rows of grey or white gravestones, of which even the neatly rounded tops seemed to imply a kind of additional finality. I looked again at the treetops rising almost triumphantly to heights that dwarfed the memorials constructed by humans. The sturdy brown trunks and luxuriantly verdant branches proclaimed the consoling continuance of living things.

I was heavily disguised. Not that this was strictly necessary, for most of the people at the graveside, even though they were my relatives, had never met me. They had all been living at the other end of the country or even abroad for very long periods. It was true I had once met Pauline Appleby, for instance, when she was much younger and happened to be over here on a brief visit from Canada, where she was born, as her father, my cousin, had settled there a long time before. I was Pauline's cousin once removed but was known to her as Aunt Doris Batley. To most of the younger generation, such as little Drusilla Lane, I was cousin twice removed. They probably thought of me as Great Aunt Doris Batley - if they thought of me at all.

My disguise was as extra precaution. Even after one has aged considerably, certain facial characteristics persist. Although the known and well-meant exclamation, 'You haven't changed a bit!' is rarely quite sincere, the more hurtful 'How you've changed! - I should never had recognised you' is often mercifully inaccurate if the speaker looks for a moment or two longer. So I applied such talents as I have to changing my appearance. They are quite adequate, since after a successful period as a beautician I moved on, with equal success, to amateur theatricals.

I cannot quite remember whether use was made of the phrase 'our sister here departed', but there was certainly a reference to 'sure and certain knowledge of the life everlasting', or words to that effect. The Reverend Colin Willard did not intone them artificially or regard them as mere routine. He was unmistakably making a sincere effort to bring his listeners comfort and reassurance. I am certain that he does this on all other such occasions. I made a mental note to send a little help his way when the time came for me to leave this world. His life cannot be easy, since owing to the shortage of incumbents he is not only the vicar at St Matthews, Allington, but also has to be responsible for St Mark's over at Upper Linley - and is dependant on his bicycle, as he and Mrs Willard cannot afford to run a car. Even so, he will be likely to sacrifice a proportion of my much-needed little legacy by making a donation to church funds . . .

It may be wondered how, in view of the long separation or even complete absence of acquaintanceship, I was able to identify a few of the mourners. This is because I eventually moved away from my tree, joined the throng and introduced myself as a 'Mrs Mary Wilgrove, Miss Batley's temporary housekeeper'. So they, in their turn, briefly made themselves known to me during the few minutes left before the vicar spoke his final words.

Having been notified of the death, partly by the said 'housekeeper' and partly by the executors, they had travelled long distances in order, I imagined, to be seen to pay their respects, and secretly all agog for the reading of the Will.

Gillian Craig was a genuine niece, without any complications of cousinship, being the daughter of my late brother Denis Batley. She had charge of five year old Drusilla whom I have already mentioned and whose relationship to her would have been a little different to work out. Drusilla called her 'Auntie Gillian'.

Should one take children as young as that to funerals? Perhaps not - but Drusilla's presence and the words I heard her utter on this occasion changed the whole of her future.

I think it was Cynthia Steadly, another distant cousin, who indulged in the atrociously hackneyed observation: 'Oh well, she has now gone to her long rest.'

A few moments later some of those present dropped nosegays down onto the top of the coffin, while others were content with little clods of soil which landed with a sound somewhere between a 'bump' and a 'plop'. And then Drusilla exclaimed: 'They shouldn't throw things down there, should they, Auntie Gillian?'

Auntie Cynthia said Auntie Doris had gone down to have a nice long rest.

'They'll wake her up!'

It is as such moments that a little child's unique blend of innocence and solicitude warm our very being - blotting out the memories of despair caused by infantile cantankerousness or cussedness . . .

And so Drusilla's golden heart, five summers young, made her as deserving in her way as the Reverent Colin Willard was in his. Like everybody else present she thought the coffin contained her Great Aunt Doris. They were unaware that the body was that of someone totally unknown and that the so-called Mary Wilgrove, standing in their midst, was their elderly relative Doris Batley, spinster, who had thus definitely not so far departed this life . . .

There were two reasons why I succeeded in being a spectator at what was supposed to be my own funeral. The first, of course, was that the people concerned, while related to me in various ways which I have partly outlined, had never really been in touch with me.

The second reason lay in something far more dramatic - an extraordinary occurrence without which my scheme would doubtless have been impossible.

A fortnight earlier, at my home, Woodside House, in Crossley Glade, I felt unwell and rang up the surgery in Allington. It was one of those group practices, as they are called. They sent a Dr Singh to see me, and I managed with great difficulty to get out of bed and go down the stairs to admit him. I then hurriedly went back upstairs, Dr Singh following in my footsteps and occasionally putting his hand out to help and support me.

He remembered me about ten days later on receiving a telephone call, apparently from a 'temporary housekeeper' whom I had since taken on. This time he was asked to certify my death, as he was able to do without the need for a post mortem, having seen me within the previous two weeks. Acting as the 'housekeeper' I let him in, and he wrote out the certificate after examining an unknown woman whose body now lay in my hall. The body he took to be mine.

Recollecting my recent illness, he seemed hardly surprised that I had since passed away. The woman looked uncannily like me, and I had known how to alter her appearance so that he would actually mistake her for the old and frail-looking Doris Batley whom he had seen on his previous visit.

This subterfuge on my part was only feasible as a result of a frightening event that in the end proved to be propitious. Not long before I had taken a late evening walk in the wood to which my back garden gate gives access. It had fortunately been quite deserted, so that nobody had seen me when I suddenly stumbled across the dead body of a woman of about my age and appearance. She had apparently committed suicide with a massive overdose of tablets assisted by a bottle of whisky.

If I wondered who she might be and why she had taken such a drastic decision, it was only for the first few seconds. Curiosity then gave place to a sudden inspiration: I could use her body to make it look as if it was myself who had departed from this world!

I first fetched a pair of gloves from the shed just inside the garden gate. There would thus be no evidence of my having touched the corpse, an extra precaution, since, after all, my fingerprints were still unique, despite my disguise. Later on I burnt the gloves.

I then dragged the dead woman all the way to my gate, hoping no stranger would arrive upon the scene before I got safely into my garden and shut the gate behind me. Once inside, I continued to drag the corpse up the path, through the French windows and into the lounge. Despite my recovery from my recent illness this took some effort. There was no way in which I could get the body upstairs to my bed, although this would have been by far the most satisfactorily convincing scene of all to which to summon the doctor on that final occasion.

I should now explain the reason for my course of action. For if the circumstances enabling me to carry out my plan were very unusual, the same could be said of my motive in hatching it in the first place.

Apart from a charity or two and the deserving man whose pastoral responsibilities included me and the few other churchgoers in the neighbourhood, I considered it a duty to leave the bulk of my considerable assets to the 'clan'. By this I mean the people who are descended, in one way or another, from my barrister grandfather, Jarvis Batley, and their husbands and wives.

That my personal association with the 'clan' was tenuous or even largely non-existent made little difference to this feeling.

As people vary widely, however, it went without saying that there would be 'clansmen . . . *and* clansmen', so to speak. Legatees *and* legatees, in other words. Yet how could I know which of them were the most deserving and which of them the least?

There was naturally no infallible way of judging the *complete* character of any of them. I decided, however, that it would be useful and enlightening to listen to as much as possible of their conversation at my funeral, at the subsequent gathering and (especially) at the reading of my Will by Mr Edmund Tracey, my solicitor and executor.

I had already made a Will some time before. Its terms took into account the 'legatees' respective degrees of relationship to me and respective financial situations. These factors sometimes conflicted. For example, Gillian Craig was one of my closest relatives, but her husband Neville Craig QC, a member of the chambers of which my grandfather had been a leading light in his day, had left her very well off when he was killed in an accident. On the other hand the Cynthia Steadly who had thought I had 'gone to my long rest' was only a distant cousin, but I had heard that she had some difficulties in making ends meet. Platitudinous she might be - a deserving case none the less.

I thus knew something of my relatives' circumstances but nothing of their natures. Over the sandwiches and sherry following the burial, however, my plan started to pay off. Pauline Appleby, for example, had tears in her eyes when she turned to me at the reception and said, 'You know, Mrs Wilgrove, I feel I miss Aunt Doris - she was a cousin once removed, really - even though I had not seen her since I was very young. It sounds funny, but even then I sensed what a dear person she was, and that sudden spark of affection has remained with me throughout the years.'

She would be 'remembered' in my revised Will to a greater extent than in the original testament . . .

Then when the Will had been read out by Mr Tracey, a great-nephew of mine called Cyril Alverton, whom I had never met before but who had always impressed me as particularly attentive at a great distance, said to Pauline Appleby:

'Well, to be quite frank, I expected a trifle more than the two thousand quid I've been left. After all, I took care to send the old bat a birthday card, Christmas card and Easter card all through those fifteen years. Or should I say 'the old dormouse bat' - you know, 'Doris Batley - dormouse bat'! Ha, ha! Ha, ha!'

I decided that here, at all events, one clause in my Will most certainly required revision. In the opposite direction, of course, to the amendment I would make in the case of Pauline . . .

After 'Mrs Mary Wilgrove, the temporary housekeeper' had called the doctor to certify 'my' body as dead, when it had been moved to the mortuary by the undertakers and eventually interred as I have described, I returned to Woodside House and got rid of my disguise. It had been very thorough, as this was a field in which, as already mentioned, I was well practised. The restoration of my original appearance was no less thorough.

Two days later I called at the offices of Tracey & Boyd and asked to see Mr Edmund Tracey. I had to 'return to life' and show myself promptly, or else the original Will, which was no longer in accordance with my wishes but was in his hands, would have been 'proved', as they say, and carried out.

'Good morning, Mr Tracey,' I said with a smile as soon as I had been shown into his private office. 'I'm just back from a short holiday. I'm so glad you're able to see me, as I'm anxious to make a new Will.'

No words to mine could even begin to describe the expression which his face assumed the moment I made my appearance. It was one of the utmost mystification and bewilderment. Had he been at all superstitious or believed in any of the ways in which the dead have been said to be capable of returning to earth, one could add 'terror'.

He rose from his desk, began to walk round it, then suddenly put out his hand and leant heavily upon it as if to steady himself and avoid falling over. The sound coming from his throat was a curious blend of gasp and croak, almost like that made by a man dying a painful death from some poison.

He then hurriedly disappeared without uttering a word, of which he would perhaps have been totally incapable.

He must have eventually succeeded in collecting himself to some little extent and then reported my incredible resurrection to his partner, Leonard Boyd, who entered the room about a quarter of an hour later. He gazed at me in astonishment but was somewhat calmer than Edmund Tracey, not having been so closely acquainted with me or personally responsible for the formalities following my 'decease'.

'Miss Batley, we can none of us even begin to comprehend what has occurred!' he said. 'Dr Singh had paid you a short visit some time before, when you were so unwell. A fortnight or so later he received a telephone call from somebody who said you had recently engaged her as your temporary housekeeper. This Mrs Wilgrove told him she had found you lying dead at the bottom of the stairs. Needless to say, she was highly agitated - almost incoherent, in fact. As Dr Singh went to your house and found the body there and as the woman was of remarkably similar appearance to you, he certified the body as yours. I then saw to it that the funeral arrangements were duly made and notified your relatives, as you had once requested me to do if need arose.'

Such was the gist of Leonard Boyd's account of the recent happenings, though it was far more disjointed and agitated than might appear from my summary.

He went on to say that some of my distant kith and kin had travelled considerable distances to be present at the service held at St Matthew's, the subsequent interment, the reception and the reading of my Will.

He then added that Mrs Wilgrove, my housekeeper had been present at these proceedings but could no longer be traced. She had perhaps made the same mistake as Dr Singh and thought the body to be my own, having only met me once before being taken on.

'Or else,' I told Leonard Boyd, 'she has played some highly bizarre practical joke - if joke it can be called. At all events she has completely disappeared.'

The body in the grave, now known to be that of a stranger, naturally had to be exhumed. It remained to be seen whether painstaking police investigations would then enable it to be actually identified.

There is nothing to connect me with what occurred; my astonishment was made to appear equal to everybody else's. I do not know the penalty for concealing a body, allowing it to be interred with a false identity, and so on, but was confident that it need never concern me . . .

The partners of Tracey & Boyd eventually regained some of their usual calm and were able to take down particulars of the revised Will and Testament which was the purpose of my visit to their offices. They could not, in any case, 'prove' and carry out the old one - since I was still alive!

The text of most Wills is probably confined to the details of the bequests, but comments on the reasons for the decisions in question are sometimes added.

The following were the main provisions, insofar as they differed from the terms of my old Will, and also the main remarks which I added to the clauses in question.

To my cousin once removed Cynthia Steadly: three thousand pounds. (Instead of one thousand pounds.)
To the Rev Colin Willard, Vicar of Allington, who has time and again been a helper and - whenever sadly necessary - a comfort to all of us in his congregation: five thousand pounds.
To my niece Gillian Craig, who is bringing up my distant relative Drusilla Lane, whose loveable character and sweet nature, even if such things are often largely innate, must nevertheless be due in no small

measure to the influence and example of Gillian herself: ten thousand pounds. (Instead of five thousand pounds.)

To the said Drusilla Lane: seventy-five thousand pounds, to be held in trust for her until she reaches the age of twenty and to be invested and used during that time for the purpose of furthering her education and also supporting her at university if she succeeds in obtaining a place there, the balance to be paid out to her on her twentieth birthday:

My property, Woodside House, Crossley Glade, Allington, and all its contents.

(The trustees would have to be appointed in due course, possibly from among my other relatives but in any case with Mr Boyd's advice.)

Lastly:

To my grand nephew Cyril Allington: ten pounds. (In place of the original two thousand.)

In this case I added:

By way of sadly inadequate compensation for the expenditure he incurred throughout the years by sending Christmas cards, Easter cards and birthday cards to his great aunt Doris Batley - the 'old bat' - or should one say 'dormouse bat'?

He may wonder who on earth it could have been who had overheard his words and repeated them to me, but he will probably not have forgotten them even if, as I hope, many further years will have elapsed before I am really dead and this new Will is read out. For he must have considered them the height of wit. When the typical life-and-soul-of-the-party-at-other-people's-expense brings forth such a little gem he usually enjoys the memory of it for years to come.

I stopped short of quoting his concluding raucous, 'Ha, ha! Ha, ha!' He may have forgotten it, for with his kind it is so automatic as to be sometimes almost unconscious.

And after all, such an important document should not be cluttered up with too many little trifles and asides - but framed with due dignity . . .

THE TIME CAPSULE
Andrew Detheridge

On the third sun of Noldon, Nossolom carefully tended the vast firterra-
leaves in his garden and hoped that the season of ice would be brief that
year. Drofreda stuck her head out of the entrance to their sprawling
dwelling and called him softly from a distance of no less than half a
mile. 'Nossolom, please do not be long. Reports have reached us of
debris storms heading this way from Seyak Minor.'
Nossolom nodded and began shuffling his considerable bulk at nine
foot strides back towards the house when the first chunks of universal
waste fizzed past him and splattered into the clay-like surface of the
planet, hissing briefly and then cooling almost instantly as the freezing
undersoil exerted its vice-like grip. Nossolom quickened his pace and
was almost at the opening, hued skilfully from the rock, when his single
eye caught sight of a silver oblong, still hissing slightly, a few yards to
his left. Tentatively touching the box, he found it had already cooled to
the touch and, without pausing to examine any closer as the space
debris was now turning into a steady shower, he plucked it from the
sucking earth and hurried inside.

With growing interest, Nossolom placed the box carefully onto one of
the circular eating surfaces that adorned the main dining area. It
appeared regular in shape and had obviously been made by some
primitive craftsman from a distant solar system. It was made of a base
metal he had not come across before, but that was not unattractive to
the eye. In the centre was an elongated hole that, he supposed, had
something to do with opening the box but, as he controlled every
appliance in his own life with thought-waves, he couldn't fathom how it
could work. Despite concentrating on it for a whole five swollips, it
refused to respond to his thoughts and so he tried a new approach - he
put six curling digits underneath the box and a further seven above and
pulled them up. The box opened with a satisfying crack and the
contents birthed themselves onto the surface top and lay there like
secrets waiting to be shared.

Tenderly, Nossolom sifted through the ancient discs as Drofreda joined
him, intrigued by his find. Together they fed the discs into the
Translator and waited eagerly for the results to appear on the Hologram

Vision. A small figure appeared and began to read out the contents of each disc. Apparently, the box had come from a distant planet called Earth, inhabited by an ugly looking breed called Humans - along with some infinitely more attractive species (Nossolom found elephants particularly aesthetically pleasing, while Drofreda thought that the animal called the rhinoceros had a certain innocent charm).

'Listen!' she exclaimed, repeating the words of the shimmering figurine, 'this capsule was buried on their planet in Dation 268 - or 2075 AD as they would have called it - I wonder what has happened to their planet in two thousand of their earth years?'

Fascinated, they listened to the history of the evolving human race, the rise and fall of insignificant Empires, the subjection of other species - even of sections of their own species - and felt a growing despondency. They were briefly cheered by a bizarre human intervention called Religion, in which humans bowed in primitive worship before an invisible entity alleged to have created the entire Universe! They were reminded of the Alluvians, who believed in Meteor Gods and told their offspring nightmare tales of sandserpents that came up out of the deserts like rockets and swallowed you whole - spitting out the bones before returning to their cavernous lairs. Still, this was even more extreme. On their own holidays, they had travelled through four solar systems, if there were strange 'gods' living in the heavens - where were they?

They were also amused by the PAD systems left in the box, that allowed them to interact with humans that had been nothing more than space dust for over two millennia. The PAD system (or Personality After Death) had been set up in the first decade of the twenty-first century. You spent a week at a PAD centre, during which time they asked you a series of questions to determine your attitudes and opinions, your hopes and fears. Computers then monitored your behaviour, speech patterns, habits and quirks, in order to produce the 'Vidiyou'. Then, after death, your ashes were scattered on the surface of your favourite moon and a photo frame was installed in your living room. At the flick of a switch, the glass in front became a computer screen and the 'Vidiyou' surged into life. Thereby, you could hold a conversation with your deceased spouse and an identical, voice-synthesised replica of them would respond, exactly as they would have!

In this way, the loss was considerably lessened and it had the distinct advantage of being easily unplugged in the middle of arguments!

As Nossolom and Drofreda got to know individual humans they began to feel a sense of warmth, of humour, of . . . 'humanity' that had been a missing link in so many other species encountered on their extensive sojourns between Milky Way and distant galaxies. They pledged to visit Earth on their very next trip and telepathically asked the computer to plot the most direct route. Strangely, the computer could not locate Earth in any solar system and so they asked the computer to chart the history of Earth from 2075 AD to the present day in order to classify the situation. 3030 AD was the last date recorded on the log. In this year, global conflict on Earth proved to be the final conflict. Nossolom and Drofreda looked at each other in disbelief as they realised that the inhabitants of a distant planet had been reckless enough, not only to destroy themselves, but their entire world. A few shuttles were alleged to have made it off the planet before the ultimate destruction, but what happened to them or if, indeed, stories of surviving human beings are merely urban myths, is impossible to tell.

Nossolom switched off the Hologram Vision with an errant thought and looked across as Drofreda. The heart of her eye burned vibrant orange and the corners paled to lilac as she cried Noldonian tears, weeping for the lost hopes of a lost race.

FINDING FLEUR
Susan Simpson

Katie hadn't had a good night. Excitement had robbed her of several hours' sleep and when she had slept it had been brief. She'd woken early and had come crashing into my room with all the enthusiasm that only a seven year old can muster. 'When are we going Mum? Can we go straight after breakfast please?'

I glanced over at the clock on my nightstand. The illuminous green LCD told me that it was 6.12am. Katie's eyes followed mine.
'Oh that rotten old clock is always getting me into trouble,' she cut in quickly. 'It must be lying Mummy, it can't possibly be that time because I've been awake for *hours*.'

In the bathroom I heard her chanting, 'We're going to get Fleur. We're going to get Fleur.'

We had been talking for some time about getting a dog. It was good for a child to have a dog and it was good for a dog to have a child. We had passed back and forth the possibility of several breeds, Paul and I fighting over our particular favourites. Katie however was above all arguments.

She knew exactly which dog we were going to get. A Fleur! Over breakfast she chatted happily about Fleur. 'Oh Mum, she'll be my lickle baby, I'll put her in my pram with dolly and take her out for walks, and I'll brush her, and love her and give her lots of nice things to eat.'

Giving up all thoughts of Afghan Hounds and Rhodesian Ridgebacks, we decided we'd go to the local Animal Rescue to *find Fleur*. We had rung in advance to make an appointment and to tell them to expect a very excited little girl who was absolutely not allowed to come away with the entire range of dogs on offer.

A very robust lady met us at the gate, five minutes before the official opening time. She took us into the office and gave us a five minute lecture on making sure we were emotionally, and financially ready for the burden of a dog. I liked her and her no nonsense attitude immediately. It was so apparent that a deep love of animals and a low tolerance of fools lurked beneath the stern demeanour.

Just when it seemed Katie could contain herself no longer it was time to go and look at the dogs. We walked across the exercise yard and were let into the dogs' domain. The smell of Jayes Fluid and urine burst through the opening pen door in greeting. We walked into a long dingy, very smelly corridor.

It was four foot wide with cages six foot by four foot to either side. Although every care was taken to make the dogs comfortable, this was not a happy place for them to be. This was no *home*, merely a prison where the victims were incarcerated for the sins of the perpetrators. The lady explained that lack of resources meant that there was a limit to how much could be done for the poor unfortunates in her care.

The opening of the door seemed to be a signal for the choir to begin. The noise was cacophonous and echoed off the stone walls and floor to bounce back and deafen them. Soprano yaps. Tenor howls. Gruff bass baritone woofs. Katie placed her hands over her ears, and for the first time looked a little bit daunted.

All the dogs were given kennel names for identification purposes. The dogs each had a spec sheet and these were slotted into a grid at the top of each kennel. The first cage to our left housed a black mongrel. 'Bob' was approximately seven months old. A collie cross who had been left tied to the rescue gate two months ago. He jumped up on the cage door scratching frantically for attention. I rubbed his nose through the mesh and crooned to him softly.
'Come on Mum. That's not Fleur.' Katie was already onto the next cage.

'Sandy'. Five year old 'Westie' bitch. Timid, not good with children or other dogs. Ideally suited to pensioner. Sandy cowered in her bed at the far end of her kennel well out of reach of probing fingers. She watched us with mistrustful disdain. A low grumble warning us that we were 'quite close enough, thank you'. This thankfully was not Fleur.

'Tottie'. Yorkshire Terrier bitch. Snappy!

'Rebel'. German Shepherd cross. Five year old. Good with children. Not to be trusted with other dogs.

'Bindy'. Greyhound bitch. Two years old. Abused and nervous.

'Scamp'. Twelve week old Terrier cross. Ideal family pet.

'Misty'. Six month old mongrel. Good with children.

So the list went on. A multitude of soulful brown eyes and needy yearning. Smooth coats, rough coats, matted coats. Cross breeds and unwanted pedigrees. Every size and colour of canine doghood.

I wanted them all! Katie however with steadfast fastidiousness, moved from cage to cage, giving each dog a cursory glance then passing them by. I began to worry that she had a picture in her head of Fleur and that *nothing* else would do. What if Fleur wasn't here?

I tried to talk her into a lovely little Lakeland Terrier pup called Kali. She was gentle and affectionate, rolling onto her back to have her tummy tickled when the lady let her out of her cage for viewing. I thought this the ideal dog for us. Katie stroked her politely and called her a 'good dog'. She giggled when the little brown fur ball jumped up and licked her nose. I congratulated myself on *finding Fleur*. The two youngsters played for a couple of minutes, and seemed to be bonding well. The little dog was a delight, full of graceless puppy character. Katie calmed the little pup with gentle patience and then bent to talk softly to her. 'I'm sorry darling. I hope you find a nice little girl to love you.'

Then she stood up; impatient for the hunt for Fleur to continue. I tried to convince her that the little brown pup was ideal for us. She was adamant that the pup was indeed beautiful, but it was *not* Fleur.

We continued to look down the cages. More possibilities jumped to be given a brief stroke of love before being passed over again.

Suddenly Katie stood still. Her eyes drawn to a cage several places down on the right. She let out a little 'Oh' and moved down the line looking neither right or left. 'Fleur,' she squealed excitedly as she knelt beside the appropriate cage.

I stopped aghast and read the spec sheet.

'Axle'. Three month old Rottweiler. Good with children and other dogs. Good house dog. This dog needs a lot of attention!

'Darling, this is a boy dog. This isn't Fleur.' It was a half-hearted attempt. I knew I was fighting a losing battle.

'It *is* Fleur Mummy. It *is*.' Katie's eyes began to fill with tears as she saw the risk of her dog being taken away from her, thirty seconds after clapping eyes on it.

'Fleur, come on boy. Fleur come.'

The huge puppy with paws like elephant's feet and skin that was four sizes too big for him looked bemused. He took a second to adjust to being addressed in such an odd manor by the little human. Then took a step forward *almost* leaving his bed, but, just as he was about to leap forward his courage deserted him. He moved back again, wanting to come, but not quite daring. Indecision! He looked back at his bed and then to the little girl patiently calling him. Then he flopped back down in an ungainly heap, his stump wagging frantically against his rump. He licked his big chops three times and then yapped. The noise was too high pitched for his big frame, and he looked almost ashamed of his lack of a butch bark. We all laughed. This pleased him and he stood, bending himself almost in two in his delight at this captive audience. He did a little dance marking time with his front paws, his plump shiny black and brown body quivering with the expectation of having those loving hands all over him. If he could just pluck up the courage. He shook his comical head. Chuffed loudly. Telling her that he very much wanted to jump all over her, but just didn't quite dare.

Katie called, 'Fleur! Fleur!' It was all too much. He bounded forward. Almost collided with the open cage door. Braced his back legs and skidded comically into Katie, knocking her onto her bum with a thump. The dog regained his composure before the prostrate child had a chance to find her feet, and leapt on her.

The ice was well and truly broken, all shyness forgotten. Puppy and child sprawled on the smelly stone floor. Each in its own personal rapture. A deep love was being forged.

'Floyd' as he came to be known (it took some persuading, but we did it) is sitting on the settee. His big old legs splayed fore and aft. He is snoring in a manner known only to nine stone Rottweilers. He's oblivious to the fact that soon he is to take his last ride in the car he loves so dearly.

He's thirteen years old now. A good age for a Rottweiler. His daughter, 'Fleur' is seven, and in pup herself with a third generation. Floyd is tired. His rheumy old eyes tell us he's had enough. He has a long journey to embark on, lots of bitches to service. Lots of fields to run.

To Katie he has taken on many roles. Horse, baby, protector, confidante and friend to name a few. He has stood beside her, watching the seasons turn her from child to young woman. He was guest of honour at her recent wedding. How Katie had wished she could be here today, but her first baby is due any day now and the long drive wouldn't have been good for her.

Now it's time to do the last thing we can for the old fella. I pick up the car keys holding back the tears. His head comes up instantly. 'Nothing wrong with the old ears eh Mum?' he grins at me, his mind five steps ahead of his old body as he creaks rheumatically off his settee.

'Come on fella, let's go for a ride.'

THE EDGED GIFT
A J Vogel

Ramsey had had too much of the Okaringa swamp. This was his third trip scraping for dinosaur bones and his haul had been meagre for the hardship of being plastered with mud and being eaten alive by leeches and God knew what else. Let the Congo go to hell. Next time he would make it to the Karroo. There were plenty of relics there, and at least he would be dry.

He packed his last specimen and drank half a bottle of Irish. Then a grunting and floundering impinged on his fuddled wits. He seized his rifle and ran out of the grass wigwam which he had spent the last three months trying to inhabit. A ten foot crocodile was dragging at somebody. A couple of close shots finished it off.

The victim was a sallow man in soiled khaki with a mummy-like cast of features. Surprisingly, he seemed quite calm.

'Thank you, Ramsey.'
'How do you know my name?'
'We know all we want to where I come from. You're not a very efficient palaeontologist, are you?'
'What do you know about it? Who are you?'
'Dr Frankenstein at your service. I expect you have heard of me.'
'The only Frankenstein I know of is a character in a novel. Made up a man out of bits.'
'That's me.'
'Please explain.'
'We're all there. All the characters you've read about. Nobody dies forever, even imaginary ones.'
'Where is 'there'?'
'Call it Ectopia. Once anything or anybody exists, or is imagined, it, or they, take shape there. Mostly bad ones, paying off their crimes. Why are there so few good people in novels? Dracula is spending a thousand years' atonement among the cannibals. Lord de Grey is shot every day as a pheasant. The Nazi SS are spending a million years among toxic gasses. Of more interest to you are all the old species you're interested in. I take human shape to help scientists. I shall be at it for the next

couple of centuries for flouting the laws of Nature. Sometimes my help is fortunate, sometimes not. I can't always control what they do.'

'Well, perhaps you could bring back a dinosaur for me, or a unicorn, maybe?'

'A dinosaur, yes, because they were on Earth. I could bring you a unicorn, but daren't. I know Nature well, and she is jealous of her powers. Anything that has been, I can reward you with, but not anything that has never been on Earth; that is for Nature to do when she thinks fit, and no one else. In human shape, I run into trouble, and would like to reward you.'

'How?'

Frankenstein handed the scientist two pots of powder. 'Light a little of the red one to call up any creature that has existed. The process takes about ten seconds. If you want to get rid of it, light a little of the blue, the disappearance will take some time. When it is finished, there will be no more, and our account will be square. One reservation. I am here to help you as a scientist, not to make money for you. Don't try to make any commercial gain, or to make the powders. They contain substances which are not found on Earth.'

The mummy face wrinkled. The claw hands waved farewell. The being was gone.

Was he drunk, or crazy? All the wet heat, the insects, the parboiled chicken and mealies, the whisky. He was going doolally for sure. He sweated. Then he realised that he was still gripping the two pots. They were real enough at any rate.

It was a long haul to the coast. Most of the time storm clouds trailed overhead, and back in Yorkshire it was weeks before he unpacked. The pots were still there. He had almost forgotten the things.

After a good drink with Fraser and Burrows, he felt emboldened to try the powder. The worst that could happen would be a stink, and he was used to that.

He put a match to some of the red powder. It burned with a bright crimson flame and gave off a sickly sweet odour.

'I want a dodo,' he shouted thickly.

A shadow formed on his study floor. Bit by bit it materialised. He stared, owlishly. The extinct bird stood before him. It squeaked, it defecated. He groped forward and touched real feathers.

'Who's going to believe this?' he muttered.

The bird opened its beak and squeaked again. He has expected a raucous screech, but it was more like the cry of a snared rabbit.

'Better feed it,' he reflected. 'Vegetable feeder, I suppose.'

He got some cold sprouts and mashed parsnips from the freezer, which the bird attacked voraciously.

'What the hell is going on?' he asked himself. 'Why stop at a dodo, why not a dinosaur?'

He went out into the garden, lit some more of the powder and called up a Brachiosaurus.

A vast shadow blotted out the sun. He gaped up in stupefaction at the huge legs. The neck swung. The tail smashed down the back fence. Old Mrs Ward, half drunk as usual, was out fumbling with washing. She screamed and fainted.

The smooth head smashed through the kitchen window. The twenty ton monster started to advance. The house would cave in like cardboard if it kept going. In haste, he lit some of the blue powder. The slow-moving creature had only advanced a few paces when it started to fade. Thank Heaven he had a hundred foot garden and had started his capers at the far end. The vast form weakened just in time and disappeared. Enormous pits were left in the dug borders, and the whole garden reeked of primeval swamp.

He went back and finished the whisky. The dodo was whimpering under the dining room table, pellets of ordure were everywhere.

He shut the dodo in the tool shed and left it food and water. The bird rubbed against him, terrified by the now-vanished monster.

'Can't leave it here,' he reflected. 'Make a hell of a mess.'

He lit some of the blue powder. The dodo faded and disappeared. A banging took him to the door. Mrs Ward's mooncalf face confronted him.

'What was that in the garden? I saw a huge animal.'

'Something in your glass, I would think,' he said. 'If you're feeling low, have a hair of the dog.'

He pushed the remains of the whisky at her and shut the door. It was lucky that there were no other witnesses. The old soak had been in and out of alcoholic wards, and nobody would take her seriously.

Ramsey loaded his rifle and packed it, the powders and a potholer's helmet in a canvas sack. Taking his suitcase, he bought a ticket for Wells and went from there to the Cheddar Gorge. Having found a suitably large cavern, he lit the remainder of the red powder and called up Tyrannosaurus Rex.

He did not bargain for what materialised. He knew the appearance of the great dinosaur from reconstructions, some done by himself, but the reality drove him insane with fright.

Scimitar teeth gaped at him. Red, predatory eyes glared down from a height of twenty feet. There was obviously no time to use the blue powder. He fired his rifle once, twice, into the beast's thorax.

With a hiss like a thousand cobras, the dinosaur charged. A huge hind claw came down on his body, ripping it open, as from the slash of a giant razor. The other massive foot crushed him into the ground, and lifting, hurled him forty feet over a ledge at the back of the cave and down, down, into the depths of a ravine, still convulsively grasping the useless rifle. The beast stumbled out of the cavern and collapsed in a mountain of scaly, bleeding hide and muscle.

Footnote:
A strange report has just appeared in the Journal of the British Museum of Natural History, which we give without comment:

'Remains of a carnivorous dinosaur have been found in one of the Cheddar caves off the usual tourist trails. The weird fact is that the bones are comparatively fresh, and pieces of muscle and skin suggest that it died within the last forty or fifty years. The cause of death is unknown, but some vertebrae are fractured by what is consistent only with shots from a high-powered rifle. Our colleague Arthur Ramsey, who disappeared many years ago, would have been particularly interested in this find, which is unique, and, to date, unexplained.'

SUMMER SMILE
Joyce Walker

Was it only last summer they had met? They had shared so much since then that it seemed impossible to believe it was such a short time ago. He'd knocked the glass of coke from her hand, making her shriek as the cold liquid splashed onto her sunburnt skin. Mercifully, the glass hadn't broken, so there was no real harm done and the offer to get it refilled for her gave him an ideal opportunity to get to know her better. It was the start of a summer romance that was to last long after the holiday was over.

He could recall quite vividly how she looked that first day, seated opposite him in a café by the beach. Her hair, newly permed, curled tightly round her face after her swim and the smile she had given him as he handed her the drink. A smile that didn't stop at her mouth, but lit up her whole face. She had smiled often then and it never failed to make his heart turn cartwheels.

Where has the smile gone? He asked himself as he stubbed out the end of his cigarette in the ashtray. How could living together for six months have changed her from the bright and happy girl he'd met, into a tired young woman whose face showed little happiness at all.

'Oh Jenny, what have I done to you?' he asked aloud, his voice echoing round the lamp-lit room. His decision to leave had been hard. The decision not to give her some advance warning, harder still, because he knew that if she'd pleaded with him, he would stay and he loved her too much to watch her die emotionally. 'Go now,' the voice of his conscience kept saying, 'while she's young enough to forget you and start afresh with someone else. Before you have children.'

The thought that they would never, now, have children together saddened him. In his happy ever after dreams he'd seen his future family running along the beach and cavorting in the sea and imagined himself telling them as he bought them ice cream from the beach café, 'This is where I met your mother, you know, and we were so much in love that we stayed together forever and ever'. He shrugged off the thoughts that were threatening to engulf him.

Looking at his watch he realised that there was still over an hour to go before he had to leave to get his train and he wondered what she would think of him when she found the note he'd put on her bedside locker.

'I love you, but . . . there's no one else, but . . .' The words seemed so hollow and he'd gone through a waste paper basket of excuses before he came up with the final version. She would probably hate him. Still, at least this way she wouldn't ask him to stay.

'Oh well,' he sighed, 'time for one last cup of coffee before I leave.' He walked through into the spotlessly clean kitchen and put on the light. Being houseproud had been the one small flaw in Jenny's character. The only thing about her that irritated him, but it really impressed his mother.

'Anyone,' she said, 'who can stop Mike from leaving his dirty clothes all over the bathroom floor, or a coat over the back of a chair, has to be an asset to the family.'

He was just pouring boiling water onto the coffee granules in his mug when he heard a movement behind him and turned to find Jenny standing in the doorway. She looked small and very vulnerable in the blue silk kimono he'd bought her for Christmas and was clutching the note he'd written.

'I was just making coffee, did you want some?' he asked, with a brightness he wasn't feeling.
She shook her head, tossing the brown curls and he noticed that tears were brimming her eyes, but hadn't yet begun to spill over onto her cheeks. When she spoke her voice wavered slightly.
'Why?' she said, holding the piece of paper out to him.
He shrugged. How could he tell her the answer to the question that had been puzzling him for the last two hours, when he hadn't reached a conclusion himself.
'Because I don't make you smile anymore,' he replied.

Her sadness and anger mingled into one and when she answered it was with some venom. 'What do you want me to do, walk round grinning like a Cheshire cat all the time?'
'No, of course not, I just want you to be happy.'

'And you think this,' she yelled, waving the note furiously in front of his face, 'is going to make me happy?' She screwed it into a tight ball and threw it into the pedal bin. 'Mike I love you,' she sounded desperate, 'and more than that, I need you.'

It was his turn to shake his head. 'I don't think you do, otherwise, we'd enjoy being together. For the last couple of months life's been anything but enjoyable.'

'I know,' she said quietly, 'it's just that I've been feeling so wretched, but it won't last, honestly. Being pregnant takes some people like that, that's all.'

It took a few moments for her words to sink in and he scanned her face to see if it was just a ploy to keep him. There was no deceit in the blue eyes that were searching his, imploring him to stay more than any words she'd uttered. 'Why didn't you tell me?' he asked.

'Because you've been acting so strangely of late. I wasn't sure how you'd react, and anyway, I didn't know for certain myself until a couple of days ago. It might have been a false alarm.'

An awkward silence followed in which Mike was considering what difference this new information made to his plans. A baby certainly put a whole new complexion on things. He looked at his watch again, suddenly there wasn't enough time to tell her what was going on in his mind.

'Let's go through and sit down,' he said, leading her, unprotesting, by the arm. Only when they were seated did he speak again.

'Whatever we decide, I still have to go this morning.'

The tears were forming in her eyes once more, and one slid down her cheek.

He cupped her face in his hands and wiped it away with his thumb. 'I gave up my job and I start a new one in London today.'

'But . . .' Her voice tailed off.

'The pay's better anyway, so it will be best for both of us in the long run.' After a pause, he added, 'For all of us, I mean.'

She knew then, that it was going to be all right. 'You'll ring me every night?'

'Yes,' he promised, 'and I'll come home every weekend, at least until I find somewhere down there for us to live.'

'Up,' she smiled, admonishing him. 'You go up to London.'

She was the old Jenny again, the one he had fallen in love with last summer.

'Up, down, who cares?' he replied, 'Just as long as we can be together.'

UNFINISHED SYMPHONY
Amanda-Lea Manning

Sophie was now in her sixtieth year and retirement had beckoned. A long deserved holiday on the Orient Express proved a happy prospect.

As she was passing through Paris, memories came flooding back. Her youth, and her first love. She had met George as a child, they became sweethearts and fell in love. George qualified as a doctor and decided to chance his luck in the States. He would set up in a practice, find a house and then send for Sophie. But he never did. Ten months later she received a letter saying he had met someone else. There had been many suitors in Sophie's life, but George remained her constant love and she never removed the engagement ring he had given her.

Paris reminded her of that crazy weekend they'd spent together. The boat ride on the Seine. Walking by Notre Dame in the moonlight, they had promised to stay together forever, it had all been so romantic. The funny little B&B establishment, they had slept all morning on their final day after a night of dancing and drinking too much wine.

She was happy then and so was George. How was she to know just a year later, George would be out of her life forever.

Sophie followed her own career in nursing, rising to Ward Sister then Matron. She loved her work and made it her life, helping people was her way of giving the love she had to others, it was unconditional. She was extremely independent and tried hard to accept, George was no longer in her life, but he would always remain in her heart.

It was 8pm and the Orient Express was speeding down to Venice. Sophie had changed for dinner, something she hadn't done for years. She was sitting in the dining car waiting for her main course when she noticed a gentleman of her years at an adjacent table.

His expression was very sombre and he spoke to no one. She felt drawn to him and after the waiter had brought her meal, she noticed he had left the dining car.

At breakfast the next morning, Sophie asked whether her gentleman had been in yet. He had breakfasted in his cabin, was the curt reply. Then she asked if he was staying in Venice, the answer was in the affirmative and Sophie felt pleased.

On reaching Venice the passengers were taken by motor launch to the different hotels, Sophie hoped the man would be staying at hers. Yet she didn't really understand why.

She settled her things in the room and went down for dinner. She noticed him sitting in the lounge bar. He appeared preoccupied looking straight ahead. She passed his table and smiled, there was no response at all. She sat at an opposite table and ordered a sherry. The man sipped his drink, his eyes now cast downwards. The more Sophie looked at the man, the more convinced she became that she should talk to him.

After dinner she went out onto the terrace for coffee. The night air was warm and many guests were sitting outside chatting. The man appeared and went directly to a table in front of him. His coffee arrived, was poured and then he drank replacing his cup in the saucer at odd intervals. Sophie had become impatient and walked over to him.
'You're on the 'Orient Express' trip aren't you? May I join you?' she asked cheekily.
He turned to tell her he wasn't very good company, but if she wished she could join him.

Sophie sat down and looked hard into his vacant blue eyes, she had seen that look before, then raising her hand gently, she passed it in front of his gaze. It was then she noticed a white cane by his side.

'My name is Sophie Peterson,' she told him.
His mouth dropped open. 'Sophie Peterson . . . it cannot be,' was his response.
'Yes, that's right, do you know me then?' Sophie asked in a puzzled fashion.

He didn't answer immediately, then when he did he was unstoppable.

He explained he was George Lawson, her George, she must remember him at least.

Sophie looked closer at the face she had loved for years, then suddenly the ravages of time began to fall away, and there he was, her George.

'What happened? I waited for you, and then that horrid letter,' Sophie replied, her voice tinged with sadness.

'This happened,' George answered pointing to his eyes.

'You're blind, I know,' Sophie answered.

'It was a judgement, I'd set up in practice, found a lovely house and was just about to send for you, then I foolishly asked Anna out.' He explained like a guilty school boy.

'I see,' Sophie said.

'One evening we went to a club and I ended up staying at her apartment, I felt guilty as sin afterwards and told her I was engaged and loved my fiancée,' George confessed.

'And?' Sophie responded curtly.

'Anna continued to pursue me, at work, at home, ringing me all day and night, she thought it hugely funny, I kept telling her it was not to be,' George told Sophie.

'Oh dear,' Sophie muttered.

'I had finished surgery one night and she was waiting for me, I ignored her but she jumped into the passenger seat. I drove her home and parked, she refused to get out,' George said.

'Then what happened?' Sophie asked.

'After an hour I got pretty mad and pulled away, I was going home and she could sit in the car all night for all I cared. I was angry and drove fast, too fast, the next second I lost control and was on the other side of the freeway and hit an oncoming car. I didn't come round for a fortnight, then they told me Anna was dead and that I would probably be blind.' George sighed deeply as if a giant weight had been lifted.

'Oh George, that is too awful,' Sophie replied reaching for his hand and squeezing it.

'They tried to save one eye, but the damage was too severe, then there was the court case, I had killed Anna, but because of my condition they gave me five years suspended sentence,' George explained.

'Sssh,' Sophie whispered.

'No, I must tell you everything. I couldn't work, that had all gone, I was longing to contact you, but felt so wretched, my blindness was difficult to come to terms with. I was depressed because of losing my career because of it. I couldn't have expected you to have been my nurse maid, we'd been so happy and because of my crass stupidity I threw it all away,' George said, his voice tired.

'George, you should have rung me, I have always loved you, I still wear your ring, see,' Sophie told him holding up her left hand without thinking.

'Have you love?' George replied, now squeezing Sophie's hand tightly.

'Did you return to England, what did you do?' Sophie asked.

'I returned five years later and ended up living with Aunt Bess in North Wales. After my rehabilitation I was given a guide dog. I didn't bring him on this trip, I wouldn't have been fair,' George explained and then went on.

'Aunt Bess had a farm. I learnt Braille and started to write medical articles about coming to terms with my blindness for The Lancet and other medical journals. I made quite a good living, then Bess died a few years back leaving me the farm. I sold it and bought a beautiful bungalow with wonderful gardens,' George enthused now.

Then he asked Sophie whether she was married. He waited for her answer.

'How could I have married when I still loved you silly?' she told George.

'Do you still love me Sophie?' George asked hesitantly.

'I told you, I have never stopped,' Sophie whispered gently.

George kissed her hand and reached forward cupping her face in his hands. 'Still as beautiful, oh God how I wish I could see you,' said George, his voice pained.

'It's maybe best this way,' Sophie replied, her hand running across a long horizontal scar on her neck, the result of a ham fisted suicide attempt after receiving his letter all those years ago.

'Sophie, will you come home with me, I am very independent, I just want to be with you, I cannot lose you again,' he pleaded.

'You never lost me George, I was always here waiting, you just didn't believe hard enough,' Sophie responded to his question.

'You'll come to Wales then and live with me?' George asked again, just to make sure.

'George we have a lot of time to catch up on, I'm not going to let you out of my sight again,' Sophie told him in a seductive voice.

A FEW MOVING THOUGHTS
Mike

There is a large removal van outside. The new people next door are moving in at last. Julie says that I must move; that I am no longer capable of living by myself. I think I never was, but luckily I never had to until recently.

There goes Mrs Brock from number fifteen. She used to be such a good looking woman. Do I look as old as that?

Julie does not remember moving here. How could she? It was because she was on the way that we moved from our little flat and bought this house over forty years ago.

My mother and father came to see us the day after we moved in and were surprised, at first, how settled in we looked. There were no packing cases stacked in the hall, no untidiness. When we showed them round they realised why. We had hardly any furniture. We had been living in a furnished flat and had only managed to buy a few things for the sitting room, some essential kitchen equipment and a bed. The bed has gone long since but some of the other things survive.

'You will be able to take your own furniture. It will be your own home,' she says. But it won't all go in one room, will it? I never thought that I would be attached to material things. There is nothing very good or valuable but all old friends and like all old friends it is not what they look like but what memories they bring back.

That first day we had gone out to buy a kitchen table which would serve as a dining table for the time being. We got one in a junk shop for a pound. 'It will do until we can afford a better one,' we said. Later, when we could afford a better one, somehow we never got round to replacing it and there it is now in my kitchen, an antique. Oh no, it did not turn out to be valuable. It is just what we thought it was when we bought it, a cheap kitchen table. It will probably go to a jumble sale and be left over at the end; the young people today want new stuff.

There is a tile loose on the roof opposite, I must remember to tell that nice Mr Everslade when I see him - or is it Evergreen?

The only thing of any value is a small picture we were given as a wedding present. I suppose I will have room for that, but I never really liked it. It is a water-colour of a farmhouse and it was given to us by a friend who was the granddaughter of the artist. He is not a household name but is known to specialists. One of his larger oils was shown on the Antiques Roadshow a while back and the owner was told to insure for £15,000. I could sell mine for a few hundred but I will probably keep it to remind me of Jeannie.

I remember when we went to buy that chest. We looked in one window and saw exactly what we wanted. I said excitedly, 'Look, Sweetie,' I always called her Sweetie, I almost forgot her real name in the end, 'Look, Sweetie, that chest, it's only £17.'

'Don't be daft,' she said, 'that's the ornament on the top. Look on the floor.' And there on the floor was the price tag for the chest - £350 and that was forty years ago! I consoled myself with being able to recognise a good piece when I saw one and we went round the corner and bought that chest there for £9.

There's that pretty little thing from number eight bringing her little boy back from school. That means she must have been living here for five years already, because he wasn't born when they moved in.

'I don't want to go and live with a lot of old people,' I said.
She laughed and said, 'But you are one of the old people.'
But she doesn't understand. I know I'm old but I don't want to live with a lot of other old people who are just as silly as I am. I like to look out of my window and see everything going on. The young folk have their lives to lead and may not want to be bothered with me, but I want to be bothered with them.

The house next door has been empty for months whilst the builders have knocked things out and built things up and replaced this and put in the latest that. It happens all the time nowadays. When we moved in, the previous owners had moved out a couple of hours before. Everything was left bare and swept clean and the boiler, an old coke boiler of course, was still lit. I had a good look round to make sure that they hadn't forgotten anything. Tucked away in the eaves in the attic I saw a newspaper. 'I wonder what the news was when that was printed,'

I said to myself. What a disappointment, it was part of the previous day's Telegraph taken up there for use in packing up.

Julie popped in earlier and was cross because I had not had any lunch. She used to laugh at me because she said I was ruled by the clock, that I used to look at my watch to see if I was hungry, whereas she used to eat whenever she felt like it. Now I eat when I feel like it and get told off by my own daughter. Perhaps I would be better off in a place where I will get meals at regular times whether I want them or not.

We never planned to stay here forever. I always dreamed of having what I called a Proper House. Not a big or grand house but one with a bit of character; not just one in a row. Then I thought we would retire to a pretty picture book little cottage. Why didn't we? I don't know, it just never seemed to be the right time.

The removal men must be nearly finished. I can't see what sort of stuff they have been taking in, but there must have been quite a lot, they have been here several hours.

I suppose that I will have to go if only to stop Julie worrying about me. I won't be able to sort everything out. I'll just have to leave everything and pretend it doesn't matter. I'll make a list of the things I want to keep and the rest can be given away or taken to the dump. I'll do it tomorrow - well soon anyway.

Just now I'm going to get myself a nice cup of tea.

THE COUNTRY SERVICE
Anthony Williams

Weekends were usually a busy time driving the country folk home, and this, the last Saturday before Christmas had been really hectic.

My bus had been packed with both people and parcels, farmers' wives laden with food and presents, young children with balloons, an old pensioner, who had obviously saved hard, struggling triumphantly with his purchase in a large cardboard box, and just as I was about to drive off a breathless young girl came aboard carrying a Christmas tree.

But it was a happy crowd, and as I drove out of the bus station I could hear the cheerful chatter of the passengers discussing their purchases and plans for the Christmas festivities.

Being a bus driver on a country route certainly has its compensations, for as well as getting to know most of your regular passengers, it was far better, especially in the summer, than driving the 'double deckers' on the city routes.

Stopping at the various villages and farms the passengers gradually alighted, in some cases I even had to help them with their parcels, and in return 'good night driver', and 'thank you', 'Merry Christmas'.

Yes, it had certainly been a busy night, and now I was returning empty with the satisfied feeling of a job well done. I glanced at my watch, I was a bit behind schedule which was hardly surprising, and I reckoned I would be back at the bus depot in about half an hour.

Thin wisps of fog started drifting across the road and I had to cut down my speed, the fog got gradually thicker and thicker until I was just crawling along in low gear.

Eventually I had to stop altogether, it would have been sheer madness to continue, I had been driving buses for years in all sorts of weather, but never in a fog such as this. I kept my lights full on for safety's sake, just in case. You never know, I thought to myself, remembering all the crashes there had been on the motorways recently. This winding country road wasn't remotely like the motorways but I wasn't going to take any chances.

After a time I got out of the bus for a smoke. The fog, if anything was thicker than ever, like a black chimney blanket enveloping sight and sound alike.

I was beginning to get worried, not so much for myself, but for my wife, and the men back at the bus depot waiting to lock up for the night.

It was then that I heard voices, children's voices, and the sound of their footsteps on the road.

Two young children, a boy and a girl both about seven years old emerged from the foggy darkness.

'Wherever are you two youngsters going on a night like this?' I asked.
'Please, may we come aboard your bus?' said the boy politely.
'Why yes of course you can,' I said.

After helping them inside I could see then that they were twins, twin brother and sister, and both tired and cold.
'Are you - are you by any chance going to Cheswood?' said the young boy apprehensively.
'Cheswood?' I replied. 'That's a couple of miles back past the cross-roads, now suppose you tell me what you are both doing, out at night and in all this fog.'
'We've been to a tea party,' said the little girl as if that explained everything.
'It was like this Sir,' said the boy. 'Mother had driven us to the Morelands, as we had been invited to their Christmas party, and she was going to collect us at seven o'clock, we didn't like the party very much so we left.'
'You left?' I asked getting even more perplexed.
'Yes, that's right, Philida and I ran to catch the six o'clock bus that goes past Cheswood and save Mother the bother of collecting us, we missed the bus so we decided to walk home instead.'
'Why didn't you go back to the party and wait for your mother?' I asked.
'Because the Morelands didn't know we'd left at all, we just grabbed our coats and slipped away.'
'So neither the Morelands or your parents know where you are?' I said.
'No, that's why we are trying to get home,' said the young boy.

'Where exactly is home?' I asked, now fully realising the dreadful anxiety of the families concerned must be feeling.

'We live at Cheswood Hall, my name is Patrick Featherstone, and this is my sister Philida, we both knew it was very bad manners to leave the party at all.'

I now knew that they were the children of the famous Featherstone family who had owned Cheswood Hall for generations.

'Please do you think you could help us?' said the little girl. 'We can pay for our fares.' And she produced some money from her little handbag. 'Mummy said I was never to spend it except in an emergency.'

Good heavens, I thought, if ever there was an emergency this was it. I could just imagine the Featherstones, who, by now would be frantic with worry, and also the Moreland family, from where they had just slipped away as the children had so graphically described.

'Now children,' I said, 'put your money away, I'll do my best, that's a promise, but in this fog it isn't safe to drive anywhere at the moment, so the best thing we can do is to sit in the bus till the fog clears enough for me to see the road ahead.'

'That's very kind of you Sir,' said young Patrick. 'I'm sorry if we are causing you any trouble.'

'Trouble, no not at all,' I said smiling, one just couldn't be angry with them, they were such polite, well behaved children.

I looked outside, the fog wasn't so impossibly thick, but I decided to wait a while, especially as I would be driving a couple of young VIPs.

'How did you manage to find my bus in all this fog?' I asked.

'I don't really know Sir,' said Patrick truthfully. 'We knew the way back home alright, but then this fog came down, and we - well, we sort of lost our way, we just kept on walking and hoping for the best, it was then that we found your bus.'

I calculated these youngsters had walked well over four miles and most of it in the fog. Suddenly I had a brainwave. 'Would anyone like a sandwich?' I asked cheerfully.

'Oh yes please Sir,' they both cried.

'Now there's no need to call me Sir, you just call me 'driver' that's my correct title, now just sit there while I get them.' I climbed into the cab and collected the sandwiches my wife had made but until now had been forgotten. 'There, help yourselves,' I said, opening the packet.

'Oh thank you Mr Driver,' said Philida. 'I was getting jolly hungry.'

I hadn't a clue what my wife had put in them, but they turned out to be cheese and pickle, and we all agreed they were very tasty.

A short while after, the fog had cleared enough to drive, and with great care, I drove slowly along the road fully intending to stop at the telephone box about half a mile further on and phone through to Cheswood Hall.

The fog drifted like banks of cloud across the roadway, one minute the road was clear, then back into the fog again. The two children were sitting quietly in the back, for I think they realised it required my undivided attention to keep going at all, and after what seemed like an eternity the phone box appeared in the headlights.

I stopped, Philida was fast asleep, so I asked Patrick the phone number of Cheswood Hall.

Going over to the phone box there was a notice on the door which read 'out of order'. I was stunned, all my hopes of informing the Featherstones that their children were safe had gone - I dashed into the phone box in the hope that it had been repaired and the telephone engineers had forgotten to remove the notice. I lifted the receiver, but it was hopeless, the line was dead, what was I to do now? I thought, the only solution was to try and drive the bus to Cheswood Hall.

It was nearly eleven o'clock and by now I could visualise frantic phone calls being made to the police, and other people in the neighbourhood in an effort to trace the whereabouts of the children.

But Cheswood Hall was over three miles away in the opposite direction, and to try and turn the bus round on this country road in these foggy conditions was virtually impossible.

Suddenly I remembered about a mile further on there was a country lane that would lead back onto the Cheswood road.

Wearily I got back into the bus and drove on, the fog was clearing a little, but my progress was painfully slow. Cautiously I turned down the country lane which was just wide enough for a bus at the best of times, and under these conditions all my years of driving experience were being put to their extreme test.

It was nearly midnight, when I finally drove through the wide gates and up the long stately drive. I pulled up in front of Cheswood Hall, my bus looking strangely out of place under the bright lights which shone from this imposing building.

The main door opened, it was Mrs Featherstone, looking gaunt and surprised at the sight of a bus parked in the driveway.
'I have your children Madam,' I said quietly.
'My - ?' and she rushed onto the bus to find them both fast asleep on the seats inside. 'Oh my darlings,' then she turned to me with tears in her eyes.
'But however did you -'
I could see she was completely at a loss for words, both from shock and the sudden relief of finding the twins alive and well.

Suddenly a car pulled up sharply, almost colliding with my bus, it was General Featherstone, who, quite naturally, had been searching round the countryside himself -
'Good heavens, what's all this? A bus - at the Hall.'
'Just take a look inside Sir,' I said proudly.
Then we all went into the Hall and I explained briefly what had happened.
'I must phone the police at once,' said the General. 'Tell them to call off the search, marvellous show, you've done a grand job.'
'Would you also phone the bus station Sir?'
'Yes, of course, of course,' he said.

Mrs Featherstone now radiant with joy and relief, took the exhausted children off to bed, leaving the General and myself in their beautiful drawing room, which was gaily decorated in readiness for Christmas.
'Now you must have a drink - whisky? Sherry?'
'Not for me thank you Sir, it's against regulations.'
'Good heavens - Mr er Mr -' exploded the General.
'The name's Martins,' I said.
'Well Mr Martins, I feel I must - on an occasion like this - I feel well, I must -'

I could see he was lost for words too.

'What I would like best of all would be a good cup of tea, Sir,' I said simply.

'Tea - tea,' then he smiled. 'Jolly good idea, we'll both have one. James,' he called to his butler. 'A large pot of tea for two.'

It was early Christmas eve, my wife and I had just finished tea when a large car pulled up in front of the house, it was the General and Mrs Featherstone, Philida and Patrick.

'We've just called to wish you a Merry Christmas,' said the General, carrying a large hamper.

'Come in Sir, all of you,' I said, somewhat taken aback by their unexpected arrival.

My wife, who had quickly removed her apron emerged from the kitchen, and after being introduced, was presented by Mrs Featherstone with a large bouquet of red roses. The General produced a bewildering array of exotic fruits from his own greenhouse, not to mention a box of cigars and a cheque for five hundred pounds to which was attached a simple note which read, 'In token of appreciation, General J G Featherstone'.

I tried to thank him, but he wouldn't hear of it.

Drinks were passed round, the toast being 'The Spirit of Christmas'.

But what really brought a lump in my throat was when little Philida came forward and handed me a large envelope.

'May I open it now?' I asked her.

She nodded.

It contained a huge Christmas card, beautifully drawn, and painted by them both.

It was a picture of a bus with 'The Cheswood Special' on the front, and on the inside page was written, 'To Mr Driver, with an extra special wish for a really wonderful Christmas. From Patrick and Philida Featherstone'.

They both looked up at me and smiled, and this time, it was I who was lost for words.

THE GREAT ESCAPE
Pat Bidmead

She closed the door quietly behind her easing the lock into place with the aid of the Yale key. Her hand was so steady that she could hardly believe it. Strangely she felt no panic and marvelled at her own courage. She heaved a sigh of relief. For months she had weighed up the pros and cons with the pros winning hands down every time; yet always she hesitated to take that final step. Now here she was throwing caution to the wind. She glanced nervously at the neighbouring windows to see if any lace nets were moving but all hung motionless. However, she carefully adjusted her silk headscarf bringing it forward to conceal the bruise on her cheek - it was best to be cautious - no need to provide the neighbours with gossip for the coffee morning and the luncheon club.

As she walked away she recalled all she had read about refuges for battered wives and nodded her head approvingly, even though she thought them slightly degrading. She was surprised that she felt no hate just overwhelming relief as she made her way to the train station carrying her small suitcase. The few things she had packed would arouse no suspicion and give her much needed time if pursuit were to follow. What nonsense - she knew it was nonsense. He would be nursing too large a Saturday night hangover for her absence to register for several hours.

A self-satisfied smile hung on her lips as she thought of his reaction when it dawned upon him that his slave and punch bag was no longer available. That would initiate a crisis as he lay on the settee watching television. But Monday morning would provoke an even bigger crisis. There would be no one to go to work to provide for his keep.

She clasped the train ticket in her hand and noticed that her fingers were white. She was beginning to feel cold in spite of it being mid-summer. Had she put everything in her case? She went over the items in her mind. Nice clean underwear - white vest, white cotton knickers with elasticated legs and a white slip with lace trimming - all ironed to perfection. A simple white dress, a pair of new nylon tights. White shoes with small dainty heels and a white matching hat. A hat meant respectability, as did clean underwear. There was no excuse for dropping standards. Satisfied that all was in order she went onto the platform and waited for the London train. It was late and she found herself growing agitated as though a few moments would make any difference. At last it slid into the station and her journey began.

At Victoria she made her way to the public toilets and emerged wearing the contents of the suitcase she had packed but a few hours before. She walked around the corner to the bus station and boarded a bus. She was at last on the final stage of her escape. Once off the bus she found herself on Westminster bridge admiring the Houses of Parliament. She climbed on the parapet and calmly took her final step to freedom.

THIRTY YEARS AGO
Stella M Taswell

The heavy metal dinner trolley was pushed slowly into the dayroom. Minced beef again, the smell mingled with the ever-present smell of urine. The porter bent to plug in the trolley, still half an hour to lunchtime just long enough for him to pop out unnoticed to the bookies.

In the vast high ceilinged room sixty elderly men dressed in a curious mix of tweed jackets and flannelette pyjamas were ready for their lunch. Some were seated, others shuffled on their sticks or zimmer frames towards the tables set with forks and spoons, for some reason knives were considered unnecessary.

Sister Taylor was in charge of both wards that day but she was downstairs with the bed patients, those considered too frail to be allowed to spend the long tedious hours up in the dayroom. She preferred to stay on the lower floor, her asthma was worsening and if she remained seated at her desk at the top of the ward, she could still supervise all her staff and see most of her patients from there. She considered that the new nurse could run about, she needed taking down a peg or two, with her silly modern ideas. Fancy wanting to change things that have worked well for years.

The newly qualified staff nurse Helen rolled up the sleeves of her lilac coloured uniform and proudly donned her frilly armbands. Today she would get the chance to serve the meal, the highlight of the day for some of the men in front of her.

Nothing had changed for years in the crumbling building; equipment no longer wanted for the local infirmary appeared to be quite suitable for daily use in the care of these vulnerable old people. Helen's constant requests for every day items, more than one waterproof pillowcase for each patient for example were met with raised eyebrows and mutterings about 'new brooms'.

Other staff members had worked for years at this hospital and they knew exactly how things were to be done. Waterproof covers had never been considered necessary when the pillows could be dried out on the radiators, well almost dried anyway.

Ken, the other senior member of staff had been a charge nurse there for over twenty years, tall and rather overweight, Ken's outstanding features were a sprawling moustache and a constant unpleasant body odour. He spent his extended coffee breaks in matron's office; both were due to retire in a couple of years. Neither wanted to make any changes or to rock the boat. What did a wet behind the ears, new staff nurse know anyway?

At the beginning of each shift Ken's first task was to connect his car battery charger to the hospital electricity supply. Another daily habit was to attempt some form of physical contact with the staff nurse. No one ever discussed sexual harassment there; Helen learned quickly to avoid being alone with Ken.

As the trays of food were passed out, Helen noticed one of the auxiliary nurses waving from the corner of the enormous room. Leaving the food trolley, she hurried over to the agitated nurse who rushed back into the toilet area. Over the low top of one of the cubicle doors she could see someone slumped in an upright position in the corner. Pulseless and not breathing, it looked as if the old man had died against the wall.

In an attempt to lower him gently to the floor Helen placed both hands under his arms and balancing on one leg, used her other foot to try to lift his legs around the toilet bowl. Thin and frail as he was, it should have been easy to get him into a more dignified position.

One of his slippers fell off and Helen noticed a bandage on his big toe. She remembered then that he was Joe Evans, one of Sister Taylor's patients. Poor Mr Evans always upset; it was rare for him to have visitors these days, in fact Helen could not remember seeing anyone by his bed since he had been readmitted over a month ago.

One more great effort and he would soon be on the floor where the proper care could be taken of him.

It was with horror that she leapt backwards when the old man swung towards her, his blue face brushing hers, his tongue cold and wet against her cheek, his eyes enormous and bloodshot only inches from her own.

Only then did she notice he was hanging from a thick leather belt fastened to the pipe above the toilet.

Somehow the sister and charge nurse appeared and Joe Evans was pronounced dead by the doctor. Helen felt as if time had stood still and although she could hear the others talking she could make no sense of what they were saying.

Lunch was still being eaten and some of the men were wondering what the fuss was about, but death was a common event for them, most were more interested in a cup of tea, tea from the large pot already mixed with milk and sugar and stirred in the pot. No one got a choice, no one ever seemed to notice.

Statements had to be written and Helen was taken to the hospital mortuary to make a formal identification of the body. With the smell of disinfectant prickling her nose Helen waited until George the mortuary attendant rolled open one of the heavy drawers and turned back the sheet covering the dead man's face. The belt had been removed from around Joe Evans' neck but small islands of raised flesh showed where the holes in the belt had been and a buckle shaped mark sat on the side of his throat beneath his chin.

Sitting in the ward kitchen with two policemen Helen asked about the inquest, routine they said, all the statements will be read and the coroner will ask a few questions.

It took years to improve conditions for the old men at the hospital. New staff gradually took over, finances were increased but still day after day, the smell of minced beef and urine mingle and Helen still has the occasional dream of a hanging man.

LOSING YOURSELF
Ise Obomhense

You ask what's my story, well I don't have a story.

'Everyone has a story girl. Me, I was my mother's pride and joy, wearing and eating the best that money could buy until I got too big and fat. I don't know what she expected from me, was I supposed to turn the other way when she offered me desserts and sweets?'

'Maybe she was trying to make you a stronger person.'

'Wrong girl, you would think so, but not my mother, she wanted a Barbie doll. Someone with good manners and grace to make her look good.'

'So you rebelled against that?'

'Oh you bet girl! Every time I ate a chocolate cake or a brownie I was rebelling, rebelling against my mother and against society. You could say I didn't follow the status quo so to speak.'

'Well I think you are beautiful, you have beautiful hair and nice eyes.'

'That's me girl, everything but the body. I ate till I dropped.'

'Why did you do that to yourself if you had everything?'

'Isn't it obvious? I didn't have everything after all.'

'What didn't you have?'

'Love my friend, that is what I didn't have. Food was my comfort from a lonely life, and I felt in control of things.'

'Don't you mean that you were out of control?'

'No my friend, in control, in control of my body. My mother and everyone around me wanted me to look and act a certain way.'

'And you didn't?'

'You bet ya kiddo, but it blew up in my face.'

'You hated the way you looked?'

'Well that was part of it. I hated what I became, what my mother and society made me become.'

'So you blamed everything and everybody but yourself?'

'It was easier that way for me. I couldn't face the fact that I had screwed up all on my own.'

'What did you think would happen? Did you think you could gain the weight and then lose it just like that?'

'I know I was really screwed up. I guess I was living in a fantasy world.'

'And now, what do you feel?'

'I feel a loss and an emptiness inside of me, which is why I sympathise with you girl.'

'Why me?'

'I sympathise with you because when I look at you I see myself. I wanted and needed attention from everybody around me. I finally realised that I was a lonely and insecure person. At least before guys were interested in me and wanted to take me out.'

'You didn't have anyone close to talk to?'

'Would you like to hang around with someone who is busy stuffing her face with every kind of food in sight. Then later ends up barfing it all up?'

'You're not kidding are you?'

'So I decided to go on a diet, and I went from a size 16 to a size 8.'

'Did things improve?'

'Not exactly, I mean I was popular and I dated the best looking and the most popular guys in school.'

'But you still were not happy with yourself?'

'No, nothing like that, I overheard a few cracks about me, and that changed my life. I heard a guy that I was dating at the time talking with his friends, and I overheard him saying
'She is so hot, but man she definitely doesn't have anything in the brain department. But that's not the reason why I am going out with her.'

'Did you break up with him?'

'I couldn't make myself do it, instead I did everything to make him stay. I didn't eat properly; I wore sexy outfits thinking that he would like me better. Of course it didn't change a thing, he still thought of me as a piece of meat. Why are you looking at me like that, what would you have done differently?'

'Answer me, why don't you answer me?'

'Don't look at me like that, I can't stand it anymore. Help me! Please help me! Someone help me!'

'Relax Stacie, don't agitate yourself. Here I will give you an injection to calm you down.'

'I don't want to relax, I am fine nurse.'

'Look at what you've done to the mirror Stacie, this is the third one you've broken this week. If you keep it up, you won't have anything in this room. We would have to confiscate everything but your hair brush and make-up kit. Do we have to take them too?'

'No you can't take my make-up and hair brush! I would look a mess, a mess I say.'

'Well if you are a good girl, there will be no need for all that.'

'OK nurse, I will be a good girl.'

'Enough babbling Stacie, we need to get you ready to see the doctor, so eat up, you need to put some meat on that body.'

'Whatever you say nurse, I will be good.'

'Eat up Stacie, just eat up, the sooner you get well, the sooner you can get out of here and get on with your life.'

SHE'S LEAVING
Ann F Bell

Holding my daughter, minutes after her birth, there began an almost slavelike devotion, to this pink, rather shrivelled little bundle.

At that precise moment I fell deeply in love for ever. Feeling her tiny fingers curl around mine. Looking up I saw the look of pure love on my wife's face. Tired as she was never have I seen my wife look more beautiful.

The pride and joy of bringing them home for the first time. How hard I had worked in the nursery, getting it ready for this occasion.

All through childhood, her first walk, the terrible two's, the even worse adolescency. Which consisted of the punk era, with pink hair, black lipstick and even blacker hair which was sometimes tinged with other colours too numerous to mention. The tantrums, tears, sulks, when pleading for things that were a matter of life or death. The endless pacing up and down, waiting for her key in the door. Broken hearts which lasted a week, followed by everlasting loves. And the student days and all the horrors that can bring. I had loved her staunchly throughout all these times. Now she was leaving me, for a very young immature male, whom I could have liked if he hadn't been about to marry my girl.

Well my wife Marion has told me these feelings are quite normal. I'm apparently suffering from a form of jealousy, as I can't accept that someone else is to become the man in her life.

What nonsense I pooh poohed the whole idea, and went into the lounge to think (this was interpreted as sulking by the way).

But now I am being guided by my wife and daughter through the arrangements (in which seems like military precision). The days are now filled with wedding brochures, flowers and guest lists. Oh also the wedding list. (Trust me you wouldn't want to see this list, it's so long).

Also this wedding is costing me a fortune. A perogative I am told, I should be happy about.

I have been dragged round every shop ever built, had my opinion asked for and had it at once rejected. What do I know about head dresses, veils, low, high shoes? I'm just a mere male is my defence.

Every day it become nearer, my mood is getting progressively worse, my speech is far from finished yet, better ask advice from the boss. No change there then.

'Could you take Simon to the pub,' asks my daughter sweetly coming to my study, 'He really needs to get to know you better Dad, he feels you haven't accepted him yet:'

'Course I have' said I as jovially I could muster 'I'm just being a typical dad that's all'

'Yes Daddy, I know' said my suddenly very wise daughter, she held her head on one side and looked at me very maternally, I was sunk once again.

'Alright' I said, 'Ask Simon if he'd like to come with me for a drink?' Then I knew how easily I had fallen into the trap.

'He's waiting outside for you dear' she said lightly kissing my cheek, skipping gleefully out of the room before I could speak. Off to another fitting I presume.

In the pub, we sat down squaring each other up.

'We've been rather coerced haven't we?' he said,

'If you're worried about me and Jane, don't be, we'll be fine, I'll make every effort to make her happy. I do love her very much.'

He seemed so young and indefensible, I began to feel a complete heel, and resolved to try harder. 'Another pint' I said.

When it was time to leave, we went our separate ways.

'See you on Saturday Mr Scott, Dad' he said hesitatingly.

Then he was off climbing into an extremely old car, which went spluttering away.

Back home I went to hide in my garden shed, taking comfort from my familiar surroundings. Sitting in my old armchair, smoking my pipe, I never heard the door opening. There she was approaching me, and came to slip on to my knee, and nestle her head into my shoulder.

'I love you Daddy' she cooed, putting her arms round my neck, as she had always done. How my heart railed against the boy who was stealing her from me, the love, envy, grief and now loss. I was feeling, seemed about to burst out of me.

'Come on I said' quickly releasing her and getting up 'Time for cocoa, I expect your mum's already in bed eh I'll take ours up.'

Everything alright now' she asked as I handed her the mug.

'Sleep tight my darling, tomorrow is a big day' and I went up to bed.

My wife was reading in bed, looking up, she smiled 'Feeling better?'

'Yes thanks,' I said 'just need to work on my speech a little bit.'

'Well goodnight dear, don't take too long' she kissed me gently, then nestling down, she was soon fast asleep.

How I envied my wife, her peace of mind, as I lay tossing and turning, dreaming of the following day. Will everything go well? Would I let my daughter down? This very thought absolutely terrified me, at long last I must have slept, for when I woke, it was a perfect sky, it seemed as though the day would be calm and serene.

Wrong again, the house was in absolute turmoil. I flew to the shed again, only to be dragged out by Marion,
'Time to get ready now,' she said, shooing me into the house. All this was done with such a placid air, she appeared completely unphased by all that was going on around.

The cars arrived and it was time to make the journey to the church. My daughter's door opened and I gasped in wonder. There coming down the stairs towards me was a beautiful vision in white. I just couldn't take it in.

'Do I look alright Daddy?' she asked me shyly, anxiously it seemed waiting for my answer.

Going to my daughter, I held both hands and just stared, words wouldn't come, but tears of love, and joy for all the years I had shared with this beautiful child.

'We've come along way you and I' said I at last. 'Now my darling, it's time for a new life. I know he'll make you happy.'

Stepping out into the sunshine, and into the waiting limousine, to say I was the happiest and proudest man at that moment, would be no exaggeration.

VICTIMS
J Walker

John was a victim of the Great War and the age into which he was born.
It did not always appear that this was the case, for when with friends he
could be both relaxed and jovial, yet he was a victim all the same. He
had joined up in 1914 at the very outset of the conflict, and when barely
twenty was in France serving with a trench mortar battery. While being
spared from having to 'go over the top' as an infantryman may have
saved his life, he was still in the front line, and by surviving there for
three years before receiving a 'blighty' wound saw enough of the hell
of the western front to be inwardly traumatised for life.

His wound was also a serious enough to put him in hospital for six
months, and what he had endured would never leave him, so that never
a night went by to the very end of his life that he was not taken back in
his dreams to the mud and filth, and blood of the western front, and
above all the fearful sound of the guns.

The war at least provided him with an escape from an upbringing
steeped in religious bigotry and intolerance, although his mind was
never liberated, and not surprisingly destroyed his religious faith. He
had after all seen little better than hell for three years, and been taught
the hard lesson that life was merely like one of the endless games of
cards that he played with his mates on the western front, with only the
shuffling of the pack rather than any faith in god sparing his life.

When he recovered physically from his wound, and returned to civilian
life, he wanted to try and make up for lost time, and enjoy being young
while he still could, even if that meant having to break with his family.
He refused to go to church, he saw nothing wrong with picture shows,
or pretty women with a hemline that no longer sank to their ankles, and
when he went dancing and sin of all sins came home drunk,
confrontation rose to breaking point, and he knew that the time had
come to leave.

His father was already dead, and though his links with his mother were
never completely broken she made it plain enough that she regarded
him as a godless person, condemned to hell if he did not repent of his
sins. He could have told her that he had already been condemned to hell

for three years but spared her the comment. He also lost contact with his older sisters and often reflected sadly that he might as well have been blown to pieces by his wound for all they seemed to care, but he was damned if he was going to change his views in order to please them.

He determined that he would have to make his own way in the world and soon enough he fell in love with and married a pretty girl named Rebecca, who bore him a son named Chris, the years passed, and while the wound in the relationship with his family never healed, he never repented his decision to reject their way of life. Then his mother died and another world conflict loomed.

It was a war that in some ways he quite enjoyed for the activity that it generated put some drama back into his existence without exposing him to the hell of the previous conflict. Yet, the sound of the anti-aircraft guns, and of bombs exploding with all their deadly force, intensified his nightmares of the western front, and by the time it had ended he was a man of 50 with his best days behind him, still plagued by memories of that earlier, more fearful conflict, and steeped in an intolerant, narrow minded view of life.

Like a true Victorian he believed that a woman's place was in the home, and that it was his wife's duty to provide for his physical needs so long as he provided for her financially and he was fortunate that Rebecca had a quiet temperament and was prepared to accept his dominating ways. She had quickly learnt that when crossed he could have a fearsome temper, and that if their relationship was to endure she would have to learn to be compliant. Those who had known him before the Great War would not have believed him capable of such anger but his capacity for it had grown with the passing of the years on the western front and never left him.

Now he was about to enter into the last great conflict of his life with a spirit as proud and stubborn as his own, and representing a more liberated age. It was Mary, his son's girlfriend and wife to be.

In the Britain of the late nineteen forties, times were hard and money was short so that commonly enough newly married couples were left with no choice but to live with parents, which was a recipe for tension.

Mary was an attractive young woman from a background far removed from anything John had ever known, and she had just emerged from a war in which she had served as a member of the Wrens. She was a modern woman of her times with her own job, and values that had taught her that women were at least the equals of men, and were to be treated accordingly.

John's home had had the shine taken off it by a bomb blast, and he expected women to know their place. The nightmares and anger from his experiences in the Great War that he had never been able to completely come to terms with, had also reduced him to a man who was indifferent to his surroundings so long as he was provided with his basic creature comforts by his dutiful wife, and to his daughter-in-law he appeared selfish, lazy, and when crossed on the slightest matter, quite tyrannical.

It was difficult for Mary to make any allowances for John's experiences in the Great War and the mark that it had left on his personality, or the narrowness of his upbringing, of which she knew nothing, and she just saw an ageing and difficult man with whom she did not want to have to share a roof.

The conflict of temperaments was so total that it quickly led to fierce arguments and John found that unlike his wife, his daughter-in-law was quite capable of standing up to him and of displaying flashes of anger that could match his own. The increasing state of unhappiness culminated in Mary leaving the home with her baby and going to stay with her sister. His son's very marriage stood on a precipice of disaster before it had barely begun, and in order to save it truce lines had to be drawn up so that after a few months Mary reluctantly returned.

For a time, and really only because Mary felt she had no choice in the matter if her marriage was to survive in difficult times, the truce lines held and somehow she and John managed to avoid too much open conflict. Yet the damage to the relationship between them had been irreparable and inwardly their mutual antipathy hardened. Then, once the economic climate began to ease, and the opportunity came to escape, Mary and Chris did so as quickly as they could.

At first the escape was only to a nearby flat but John and Mary were still grateful to see less of each other, and once she moved a mile or so away to a nicer part of town they never saw each other again. Just as John had become estranged from his own family as a young man he now found himself estranged from his daughter-in-law to an extent that damaged the quality of his relationship with his own son and grandchildren, for Mary did not want him in her house at any price, and his son being much like his mother in temperament was prepared to accept this.

History was repeating itself and they were all victims.

More than a decade passed and the sound of guns continued to echo in John's head every night, and even during the day whenever he increasingly fell asleep sitting in his easy chair after lunch. While as pensioners he and Rebecca also sank into relative poverty, Chris and Mary began to enjoy the prosperity of the new age with the comforts of a large house and a pleasant life style.

John would have liked to visit his son's house only a mile from his cramped flat but he knew well enough that Mary would not tolerate any such notion, and excluded him as much by the strength of her personality as he dominated Rebecca by the strength of his. They were indeed like two equal forces repelling each other by the sheer stubbornness and pride of their characters.

John remained outwardly healthy well into his late seventies, and one of his last acts before sinking into his final illness was something that he had been meaning to do for a long time, which was to walk to Chris and Mary's expensive detached house that lay such a tantalisingly short distance away.

It was a summer's day and there was no hurry, but he had over-estimated his strength, and as he began to trudge uphill towards the house he found himself tiring terribly. He knew the number of the house well enough, but now breathing heavily and sweating profusely, almost thought that he was going to collapse before finding it. He had never felt quite so tired since the now far off day in the Great War when he had received his 'blighty' wound, and leant grateful on a gate post admiring his son's house with its attractive rear garden that he could just glimpse through a side gate.

He would have liked to have been welcomed, to have taken his ease in the company of his son and now grown-up grandchildren, but it was not to be. At least he still had the consolation that they visited him regularly enough, and half fearing that the front door of the house would suddenly be opened, and that his strong willed daughter-in-law would come striding through it, he soon retreated the way he had come.

The return journey was all down hill but by the time he had climbed the stairs to his flat, he was very, very tired indeed, and quickly sank into his final illness. Rebecca tendered to him with dutiful care as she had done for 50 years, exhausting her own failing strength, until finally he had to be taken into hospital riddled with the advanced stages of cancer.

By some cruel fate, Chris and Mary were on holiday when this event took place, and all the doctors could do for John was to cut him open as the shells had once cut open and killed so many of his mates on the western front, in order to seek to remove the cancerous growths. It was a pointless, unintentionally cruel exercise that left him to sink into a painful death within a matter of hours.

He died at the break of dawn, just as many of the infantrymen he had known had died in their dawn attacks on the western front, still with the sound of guns echoing inside his head, and too sunk in pain to have any regrets. More than half a century had passed since the guns had fallen silent on the western front, but now wounded as so many of those who had fallen there had been fatally wounded, John heard the sound of the guns for the last time and went to join them.

Suffice it to add that Mary did not attend his funeral.

GREECE ON CRUTCHES!
Shirley Williamson

I discovered that Greece is the most beautiful country, with the friendliest people, quite a long time ago. My opinion only rose, the year I had been doing a mad Irish jig to my friend Julian's expert violin playing in our local pub!

The carpet refused to let my flying feet, glide elegantly, as I zoomed at 70 miles an hour along the front of the bar. As my right foot stopped short, my body carried on and with an almighty crack, my ankle broke!

Seven weeks on my plaster was to be removed, so we booked a holiday in my beloved Greece. Knowing the dangers of unlit roads and rough unknown territories I decided to take my, now familiar, crutches with me. My first brand new experience came at Manchester Airport, where, upon sight of my crutches, a porter and wheelchair where summoned. They whisked me away as our suitcases slid off into the unknown.
'Would you like to go for coffee madam?' asked the porter.
'Yes please that would be lovely, but may we stop at the loo first please?' I asked.

He promptly took me to the ladies and handed me my crutches. On my return he was poised waiting for me outside the loo. I could get quite used to this I thought, as he whizzed me off again.

We stopped for coffee where he left me with my partner, Roger, who had been running behind us carrying both sets of hand luggage.

One of which (unbeknown to me) had been dropped. In this particular bag was our 'Emergency' brandy bottle, which promptly soaked its contents into our box of teabags! We decided not to throw them away and have lovely brandy tea each morning of our holiday!

On our arrival in Greece I was met once again by a porter and wheelchair. The burly Greek porter whisked me away, passed everyone else and straight through passport control, with Roger in hot pursuit! Delivered by taxi, to our apartment the lady met us with great anguish when she saw my crutches, as she had just mopped the floor!

I must say, in all this, I felt such a fraud as I didn't really need my crutches now. but you try explaining that in Greek!

1st Day in Greece:
Emerged from bed and had brandy tea together. Slipped elegantly into thong bikini and beach wrap. Grabbed crutches and proceeded to beach. Observation: Somehow does not gel, bikini, wrap and crutches.
Tried to negotiate sand and sunbed without breaking other leg or crutch! OK settled, fine. Tuck crutches under sunbed to prevent third degree burns from red-hot metal crutch!
Excellent, rays beat down, soak up sun.

Maybe had better turn over, now, this is not easy when trying not to put weight on weak ankle!

With much very unelegant manouers, have made it. Thirty minutes on other side. Gosh it's hot . . .

Decide to take first plunge in sea. Roger comes with me for support. Down sand. OK, into water, (Gingerly) then oh no, bank of stones and pebbles leading into sea. Hobble in, (very wonkily).

Clutching Roger desperately, past hazards. OK, have lovely swim! Now, normally emerge from sea to beach like Ursula Andress in famous Bond film, (or think I do!) but now decided better to sit down on pebbles and emerge backwards on bum!

So wobble on to beach like arthritic walrus! OK maybe no one noticed . . . back to sunbed.

Tea time, shower, rest, dress for evening.

Roads are OK but take crutches just in case. Up steps into Taverna, OK sit quietly at table so as not to draw attention (as still feel fraud) crutches, leaned out of sight crash to stone tiled floor noisily bringing all eyes (and waiters) to me. I nonchalantly order two Amstels and menu's. Rest of evening smooth and pleasant following more Amstels and Metaxa (Brandy) wobble home, carrying crutches mid air.
Observation: Alcohol makes one relax!

Week 2: After more of same, go on boat trip. Everyone boards boat including Roger, who I pass my crutches to, so I can board. On seeing crutches, three handsome Greek men alight from boat and insist on lifting me on. (And off, and on, again, all day.) Decide, crutches in Greece is good!

More lazy (yet hard work) days on sunbed and in sea.
Observation: Hooray, see another lady emerge from sea on bum! Find later she has had hip replacement when after sitting at sea edge for 1 hour, waiting for husband to return from snorkelling, to pull her out!
(I thought she was just sunbathing!)

Love to people watch, while lying on beach. New people come now, (White ones!) Now feel golden brown and beautiful! (until try to stand). Various shades of skin and swimsuits, vast varieties of shapes and sizes of bodies. While people relax, floating serenely on sea, I desperately try to dip my head in, backwards, to cool off without wetting my face (as it burns in sun) while keeping feet firmly on seabed!

Observation: Have decided am not maybe so elegant on holidays. Hair stands up like startled, blonde hedgehog, normal skin does not fit anymore, now full to capacity from Taverna food and Amstels, Metaxa and litres of water! Ever expanding waistline of golden coloured 'fat bits!'

Day 13.
Enough lounging like beached whale. Taverna time. Also storm coming in. Large spots of rain on beach, head for favourite Taverna.

Observation: All English people have favourite things. Chairs, pubs, tables etc.
Take up crutches and head for 'Green Paradise' Taverna (Where Mr Bean works!)
Here comes 77 year old Giannis and his wife. Having heaved her out of the sea, over the pebbles, singing and whistling, as always, Giannis dons a torn straw hat and flip-flops. They head for taverna. Mrs Giannnis (We don't know her name) swim suit sticks to her ample bum. Greek music plays, mixed with sounds of Rod Stewart and Cher, floating down from various tavernas. Tuck crutches under table away from lightning now flashing all around us!

Look out to sea, no snorkels now erect in water.

Mr Bean and his brother, scan the skies and the horizon for boats and beach for umbrellas (and people who have not yet paid for collapsing sunbeds.) We wrap beach towels around us against most unusual chill. Towels are stiff as boards from 2 weeks salt and sweat!

Mr Bean 'rushes' to serve us in typical Greek fashion (You must order food 2 hours before you are hungry in Greece!) But the Amstel appears quite quickly, so you drink thirstily. Eventually one Greek salad arrives, though, now can see two, after too many Amstels on empty stomach! 'Excellent, we must do this at home' we say every year (till you get home and back to work, and routine interferes).

We share our Taverna with Giannis and his wife and several English people, sheltering from the storm, for four hours. On our penultimate day in Greece, it's a cruel reminder of going home to English weather! Even Mr Bean scratched his head (as is typical) but the English, in true Dunkirk spirit, made the best of a bad situation, emptying the Taverna of Amstel, Metaxa and chips and eggs. Bringing Giannis and his wife into conversation, as English do. We find he is 77 and she is 63 and come from Athens.

'Never backward at coming forward' as we say in Derbyshire. The first thing the English ask them is 'Where are you from?' and 'How old are you?'

Pause: For Mr Bean to bring eggs with potatoes (chips). Wasp alert! And Taverna cats appear from thin air!

'Eggs with cheeps?' enquiries Mr Bean.

'Yes please, and may we have two more Amstels?' I ask with already giddy eyesight.

'Two Amstels' repeated Mr Bean, holding up thumb and first finger, for two!

We devour our cheeps with eggs and Mr Bean returns with two Amstels.

'There are from me, Arris.' he says Arris, 'Mr Bean' is really called Arris. We find, after coming here every day, bar two, for two weeks! (but he'll always be our Mr Bean to us).

Pause: For botany inspection of green creature, which had landed on my leg, from our favourite tree!

Fascinating, the crickets chirp once more, now rain has stopped, hidden well in our tree. Basil and herbs smell sweet after rain. Flowers bloom. Sea is aquamarine again, and if bloody cricket would shut up, would be peaceful and quiet!

Even wasps collapsing after sharing our Amstel!

Last day:
Oh well, last chance for sun bathe before homeward journey.

Observation: Do feet know when going home? Swell up like Grannies ankles!

Must cram everything in now, last time under favourite tree. Must get nicotine input before flight and very unrelaxed Manchester airport. Sun's rays, ozone, breathe deep. Oh God. First signs of peeling! Must get brown layer back in next twenty minutes (it would be on my boob!). Quick glug of water from iceberg in our bottle almost breaks my teeth! (Heaven)

Peeling, limping, toothless, I shall glide from our plane on my wheelchair!

Final observation: Only ever one seagull in Greece! Have discovered, if lie on sunbed upside down, can get nose and backs of legs brown at same time!

INVISIBLE FORCE
Phyllis L Stark

They tried to radio back to base, but to no avail. Something was drastically wrong. The controls on the small specialised aircraft had suddenly ceased functioning. They were losing height. The aircraft was plummeting downward. 'What's happening?' cried Ed the pilot.
His co-pilot Sam replied 'The controls are not working. It's as if the plane has a mind of its own.'
They tried to gain some height but were unsuccessful.
'Try the emergency controls' said Ed. 'That should do it.'
'It's no good' said Sam. 'Nothing is working. I don't know how we're going to get out of this one Ed.'
They were both worried and puzzled.
'We'll have to think of something fast Sam' shouted Ed 'or else we've had it.'
It felt as if they were being drawn downwards with a great force. They were flying over a large area of vegetation. It was dark and all they could see was a circle of light underneath them. They could do nothing but brace themselves for the inevitable. It came remarkably quickly, then there was oblivion.

They had been on a special mission flying over the jungle, testing out new and highly classified equipment. Flying conditions were good. Ed and Sam had been friends and colleagues for three years. After this mission, they were both planning a holiday with their partners, Carla and Josie.

Mission Control had been in radio contact with the aircraft until the last few seconds. Everything seemed to be going well. They knew the exact position of the aircraft and knew Ed and Sam were ready to test the equipment. Then there was silence. They were gravely concerned, not only for the lives of Ed and Sam, but also for the highly classified equipment the aircraft was carrying, which Ed and Sam were testing. If that got into the wrong hands, well, it didn't bear thinking about. Len, who was in charge of the mission, knew there would be recriminations from 'on high', as the automatic abortive procedure, which would have automatically blown the equipment into minuscule pieces, had the need arisen, had not been perfected, so couldn't be put into operation. Now they were regretting their haste.

'What do you think has happened?' said Len to his Chief Engineer Harry.

Harry was at a loss to comment.

'I just don't know' he said. 'There must have been a fault of which we were unaware. Heads will roll for this' he replied.

No reports had come in of a plane crash.

Meanwhile, Ed and Sam regained consciousness. They were in what looked like a small hospital ward, surrounded by machines. Apart from the equipment, the ward was quite sparse and pristine and looked terribly high tech.

'Thank God we're alive' said Ed. 'How do you feel Sam? Anything broken?'

'Everything seems to be OK' said Sam as he attempted to move but to his horror, found he couldn't move a muscle. 'Hey Ed,' he cried' can you move about because I sure as hell can't. All I can move is my head.'

'I'm exactly the same' said Ed. 'If we've got any injuries then we certainly can't feel them' said Ed.

'Perhaps we're paralysed' thought Sam.

They shouted but no one came. There was just an eerie silence.

'Something's not right here' Ed remarked.

On closer inspection, they realised this was no ordinary hospital ward. They manoeuvred their heads as best they could to try and observe their surroundings.

'I think we've been captured said Sam 'but by who, I wouldn't like to think.'

Back home family and friends were waiting eagerly for news of Ed and Sam. The search was continuing.

Ed and Sam were desperately willing themselves to move. They went over the last few minutes before the plane crashed. Everything had seemed normal. All the controls had been working.

'This is the work of someone whose knowledge is far superior to ours. Otherwise, how could they have forced the plane down? And how could all the controls fail to operate. One control not functioning, we could understand, but not all of them.'

The plane had been thoroughly checked over before leaving base. The only thing they remembered was the circle of lights as they were plummeting downward. Had the plane been deliberately brought down and if so, where were they and why hadn't they been found?

'We weren't flying over enemy territory' said Ed.

'It's not as if we were spying' said Sam.

Ed opened his eyes and wondered what all the plants were around him, then realised he was actually lying on the ground outside, with the blue sky above him.

'Sam, wake up' he said.

Of the plane, there was no sight, nor of the 'hospital ward'. They were dressed in their flying suits, there was no sign of the white gowns they had been wearing, but more importantly, they had full movement of their limbs.

'We're still alive and we can move, and there doesn't appear to be a scratch on us' said Ed.

'We've got no visible injuries' said Sam. 'That's strange, to have escaped a plane crash with no wounds. And why did they capture us and then release us unharmed?' 'Where is the plane?' Sam said.

They asked these questions over and over but could find no conclusive answers. It was beginning to seem like a nightmare.

Meanwhile the search party discovered the plane. It had been cleverly hidden and disguised by a huge tarpaulin, with a design on it resembling the undergrowth, so from the air it wasn't visible. It just merged with the vegetation around it. It was in tact. On further inspection, they found nothing on the plane had been damaged, inside or outside. It was a though the plane had made a proper landing.

As they thought, the equipment had been removed, obviously that was the sole purpose of the landing. But where were Ed and Sam?

They continued searching. Ed and Sam continued to trek it on foot and after two days, they were eventually found, and to everyone's relief, apparently, they were none the worse for wear.

Back home they were taken to hospital and given a thorough examination. Nothing untoward was found. When the blood samples came back traces of an unfamiliar substance was found to be present, indicating they were drugged, but the type of drug could not be identified. The doctors and scientists had never seen this substance before - it was totally alien to them.

Len remarked to Harry 'We'll have to keep this under wraps. News of this must not leak out. If the public get wind of aliens hijacking the plane then all hell will be let loose. Top security for this one.'

An investigation was carried out over a large area of vegetation and every object found was analysed and tested. The only thing they discovered was that a large area of vegetation had been flattened, by an immensely large round object, and which, to all and sundry was fairly obvious, had been a spaceship.

Ed and Carla eventually went on their long awaited holiday. It was glorious to lounge away the hours relaxing in the sun and after a few days, Ed seemed his normal self - only he wasn't. Carla noticed how very erratic and strange his behaviour was. He would do or say something, then completely deny he had ever done or said it. Carla decided to overlook this, as he must have been more stressed that she realised. She remarked 'You do feel alright Ed, don't you? You must tell me if you're feeling unwell.'
'I'm feeling fine' replied Ed. 'Never felt better, honestly.'
She assumed all he needed was rest and relaxation for a couple of weeks and a break away from things. It would take time she thought. After all, it must have been very traumatic.

However, things got worse. She discovered he was getting up in the middle of the night, and would stand on the balcony, seemingly talking to himself. She was careful not to wake him in case he was sleep walking but guided him gently back to bed. The next morning, he had no recollection of what had happened in the night.

As soon as they got home, she would insist he had another thorough medical check-up, and this time, a brain scan as well. He was just not himself.

Another frightening incident occurred this time even more scary. They had hired a jeep to drive into the mountains. It was a balmy summer day and Carla was determined to forget all their troubles for the time being and enjoy herself. Ed was driving, slowly at first, to take in the scenic view. Then, for no apparent reason, he began to speed, along the windy tortuous roads, going faster and faster. Carla was nervous.

'Ed, slow down' she shouted - but he was not listening. He was like a man possessed and had a glazed expression on his face, almost as though he was hypnotised. That was it Carla thought, he must be hypnotised. 'They' must have hypnotised him.

She decided she had to act quickly before they were both killed. She began to talk to him, slowly and gently, as though she was talking to a child. If he could hear her voice he may snap out of it. She said, 'Remember the day we met Ed, how we literally bumped into each other?' Carla went on and on about anything that came into her mind to remind Ed of past happy shared memories. Very gradually, Ed began to ease his foot off the accelerator until he was back to normal speed. Carla breathed a huge sigh of relief.

All too soon the holiday came to an end. Back home, Carla immediately made an appointment for Ed to see the consultant. Ed wasn't too keen to go, saying he felt fine. 'Carla, there's no need for me to see a shrink, I told you I feel fine.'

But Carla wasn't taking any chances. She was wondering how Sam was and learnt he too was behaving strangely.

The results of the brain scans were on Carla's desk. She just couldn't believe it. Ed and Sam needed to be operated on to remove a very small 'object' which had, somehow, been planted in their brains. It seemed too bizarre to be real. There were no scar marks on their heads. How had an object as tiny as that been planted in their heads, leaving no marks whatsoever? Carla remarked to her colleague, 'This is so unreal, so illogical, not humanly possible. How could someone do that? To actually insert a tiny object in the skull, leaving no marks whatsoever.' It was beyond belief.

Obviously, all this information was withheld from the press and general public. 'They are obviously a far superior race than humans, to be able to come and go almost undetected, so what could they possibly learn from us?' declared Len.

The operations on Ed and Sam were successful and their behaviour returned to as it was before their frightening experience.

As to the small 'objects' which were planted inside their heads - they were, as far as the most eminent scientists and doctors could determine, tiny video cameras, obviously relaying back to space, every place Ed and Sam went, every moment of the day, every conversation that took place, in fact, every single thought and movement captured. 'Quite frightening!' remarked Harry. 'To actually get inside the minds of humans. It beggars belief!'
But how it was relayed back to space, they just didn't know. It was all too much of a mystery and one which, they had no possible hope of solving, not in this century anyway.

LIGHTLY TOASTED - RICHLY ROASTED
Judy Hopkin

It was the last day of January. The weather had been flirting with the seasons and couldn't make up its mind whether to settle down with winter or spring. My new year's resolutions were a distant memory but I still felt guilty about them. I was just contemplating the merits or otherwise of an evening class in Thai cuisine against those of Tai Chi, or succumbing to the temptation of a very high calorie comfort zone, when the phone rang.

'Allo. It is Madame Gervaise. Do you remember me? I stayed with you in September.'

'Yes, of course,' I lied, thinking back furiously over the parties of French teachers we had entertained. She sounds nice, perhaps she's that charming classroom assistant who insisted on helping with the chores and declared that she never wanted to go home. Or maybe she's the 'plate' lady, an avid collector of antiques from the Portobello Road. She seemed a bit hard-edged but some weeks after her stay, she sent a huge box which on inspection contained an old-fashioned tiered cake plate, not an antique but a modern version with a rustic design. I couldn't imagine using it but it was a kind thought.

Neither of these seemed to fit the voice, so who was it?

'Do you do bed and breakfast?'

'Yes I do.' Well I do now. 'When do you want to come?'

It had been a lean month and the money would come in handy.

'We'll come on Saturday. We'll come on the Eurostar and be with you between 10 and 11 o'clock. We just want one room.'

'Will you want dinner?'

'I'll ask my friend and phone you later.'

I tell my husband.

'It's the 'plate' lady,' he said gloomily. 'I really didn't take to her.'

Later that day . . .

'Allo. It's Madame Gervaise. We're not coming on Saturday morning, we'll come to dinner. What time will that be?'

'Is seven o'clock OK?'

'That's fine, we'll see you then.'

Oh hell, now I've got to cook dinner for French people! That always makes me nervous. Why didn't I keep my mouth shut? What on earth shall I cook? Well, they're bound to be late, perhaps I'll do a chicken casserole, that will keep.

Frantically I tidy the house and make up the beds. Now for the casserole. Tart it up with some button mushrooms, that will do, and I know, slosh in that drop of wine that's left. Now we're getting somewhere.

Seven o'clock, ten past seven and surprise, surprise, a knock on the door. An attractive young woman stands there smiling. Oh yes, I do remember her.

'Allo, how are you? I've brought this for you.' She holds out a beautifully wrapped metal candle holder.

How lovely. I remember now, her name is Gabrielle. Her companion is bending over a holdall from which appears a bottle of wine. Her friend turns out to be a man, not the girlfriend I expected. But hang on, I recognise him, they came in the same party in September. But were they a couple? I must look puzzled because she says quickly,

'This is to drink in two years' time.'

Like a conjuror he produces another bottle.

'And this is to drink now,' she translates. He speaks no English but smiles a lot.

Have I made a mistake? Perhaps they want separate rooms. Never mind, I'll play it cool. I show them upstairs, they both go in the first room and plonk their bags down.

'That's fine,' she says smiling broadly.

So that's that.

'Dinner in ten minutes?' I say hopefully. The casserole won't last forever!

There's definitely something funny going on here. Now giggles and thumps drift downstairs . . .

At half-past seven I send my husband upstairs to announce that dinner is on the table. Soon afterwards they appear, flushed and breathless.

Soup is brought to the table, but Jacques insists on savouring a whole glass of the wine he brought, which we had hastily chilled. By which time the soup is stone cold. Well that's a good start!

The casserole is good, though the carrots are a bit crunchy. Not bad overall. Gabrielle chatters on, Gabrielle translates. Jacques understands but cannot converse but makes attempts. He's sporty, so is my husband, so they converse in football-speak, which is a universal language.

The apple sponge is a success, one of my better efforts.

After dinner, exhausted by the effort of cooking and conviviality, I suggest they visit the pub and thankfully they depart. I clear up and fall into bed. They want breakfast at nine and I suppose a cooked breakfast will be expected. Now my husband is brilliant at continental breakfast, which is what school parties usually get and I get to stay in bed. But cooked breakfast is not his strong point.

So nine o'clock comes and goes and I'm ready with my frying pan.

At ten o'clock they appear sleepily and sheepishly and I'm on a caffeine overload.

Breakfast is consumed at a leisurely pace, which they hold hands and gaze into each other's eyes.

At eleven o'clock I go for a lie down.

They go to the kitchen to confide in my husband. They have left their respective partners and they're going to set up home together. Oh dear!

At twelve o'clock they're ready to depart for home via Covent Garden. Good luck with the parking I say!

Then it's hugs and kisses all round and 'What wine would you like us to bring you next time?'

And then they're gone.

Well, how extraordinary and very bizarre.

Why come to us when they could have stayed anywhere in London? Then it occurs to me, perhaps they fell in love last time they came to stay!

At three o'clock the phone rings.

'Hullo.'

'Bonjour. Est-ce que je peux parler à Mme Gervaise? Ici M Gervaise.'

(Hullo. Can I speak to Mrs Gervaise. This is Mr Gervaise.)

Now who can this be? Her father, her brother? I try to summon up my abysmal French.

'Je suis désolée, elle a déjà partie.' Not bad eh?

(I'm sorry, she's already left.)

'Est-ce qu'elle reviendre, savez vous?'

What! Hang on, what is he saying? Oh yet, I get it.

(Do you know if she's coming back?)

'Je regrette, je ne parle pas Français très bien.'
(I'm sorry, my French is not very good.)
There is a long pause. He speaks very slowly.
'Puis, est-ce quelle ne me reviendre jamais?'
Oh dear, this is not her brother or her father. Jamais - that means never!
Let's work this out. Is she never coming back to me? That's what he's
asking.
I don't know what to say.
He repeats the question.
Oh, I know I'll act stupid.
'Je regrette, je ne comprends pas.'
(I'm sorry, I do not understand.)
'Oh,' and a long silence.
I can't cope with this, but how to bring it to an end.
'Pardonnez moi, je doir parti! A'voir!'
(I must go, I'm sorry.)

Later that evening . . .

'You know that sauce you made for the chicken? It was delicious.
Where did you get it from?'
'What do you mean where did I get it from?'
'Well, was it from Marks and Spencer or where?'
'What a cheek, I made it myself! Why did you think I bought it?'
'Well it had baby mushrooms in it. Where did they come from?'
'I carefully picked them out at Sainsburys, that's where. Would I
cheat?'
Sacre bleu, cordon bleu and other French curses! Men! C'est la vie!
(That's life.) It really is.

BITTERSWEET CHOCOLATE
Sandra Curtis

David picked up the phone and dialled the number written down in front of him. Sarah sat nervously by his side, tapping her foot against the side of the table leg.

'Good morning. My name is Burrows.' David introduced himself to the woman on the other end of the phone. 'I know this is highly irregular, but my wife and I are only in the area for today and driving by, we noticed your property is up for sale. So we popped along to the estate agents . . . Yes, Websters, that's right. Anyway, they tried to ring you but got no reply . . . Oh really. Well, being that we don't have much time, Websters kindly gave us your number direct, to see if we could contact you. You can check us out with them if you wish . . . Oh thank you, well you can never be too careful these days, can you? Anyway, we were wondering, would it be possible to come and view say around three or four this afternoon? Oh, I see, you're out then. Well, what about six o'clock? We really are interested and . . . You can. That's wonderful! 'Til six then. Bye for now.'

Ruffling Sarah's dark curly hair, he smiled down at her.
'Well?' she asked impatiently.
'I suggest,' David answered, as he leaned back in the settee, 'a lovely cuppa before we go and view this wonderful house. Wouldn't mind some of those chocolate biscuits either, whilst you're up,' he added, winking at her. 'Got a lot of things to do and organize before today is over.'

At about five-fifteen, Ellen Munson drove into her driveway. Time for a quick cup of tea before those people arrive, she thought. As she stepped from her car, she noticed the front door slightly ajar. Strange, she mused to herself, the kids would be over at Sally's 'til seven tonight, and Tom, her husband, wasn't going to be home 'til nine at the earliest. She walked into the hallway.
'What on earth!' she screamed. 'Oh my God.'

'Of course, I doubt if Burrows is his real name,' Sergeant Padbury explained to Ellen. 'It's an old trick I'm afraid Mrs Munson. They ring up, pretending to be interested in buying your home, make sure you're out at a certain time and come and clear your house of furniture and valuables. This is the third one we've had this week in the area. You've rung your husband of course? Good, well then I suggest a nice cuppa for Mrs Munson, Constable Drew and er . . . if there are any chocolate biscuits in the kitchen . . . ' he winked at the constable, 'Always helps you know, chocolate, very therapeutic.'

By midnight, Ellen and Tom Munson were in bed. Statements had been written and items stolen logged down by the police.

Four miles away, Sarah and David Burrows drew up outside their rented flat, after having been celebrating their week's achievement. On locking their old beaten up Fiat, David drew Sarah into his arms. 'From tomorrow my love, all this will change. I'll drive the van down to the West Country tomorrow, and from then on no more old bangers for us, no more poky little flats, no more worries.'
Sarah smiled, 'Yes, today's little job was the best of the bunch. We can't go wrong now Dave love, we've got it made,' she agreed.
'Right then, you go up to the flat,' he whispered, 'I'm just going to check over the goods.'
Giving him a kiss, she hugged him tight. 'Don't be long then love, I'll put some coffee on.'

Dave whistled happily as he walked over to the block of garages round the corner. The hired van sign shone in the moonlight. He walked over to unlock the back doors.

Upstairs in the flat, Sarah hummed to herself as she got the rest of the chocolate biscuits out and stirred the mugs of coffee. This really was their last chance to make a new start. She thought, no more scrimping and saving, no more dead end jobs. The baby she was expecting would have everything they never had as youngsters.
Hearing the front door slam, she picked up the tray of coffee and biscuits and turned towards David entering the kitchen. He stood in the doorway, his face ashen.
'It's gone, it's all bloody gone. Some lousy thief has stolen the lot. We've been robbed Sarah love. All our week's work taken, there's nothing down there but an empty van,' he sobbed.
Sarah stared at her husband stunned. Putting the tray down on the kitchen table in front of her, she visualized how their life would now be. Picking up one of the chocolate biscuits, she took a very large bite.

SALT OF THE EARTH
Margaret Kaye

White, floating marbled clouds under a clear blue sky hovering over a still sleeping village on a Sunday morning. A church bell tolls not far away, calling the early worshippers. A lone dog barks too still, just for a moment, the chattering and happy birds.

A creak of a gate and quiet footsteps slowly pass by.

At a cottage window the curtains part slowly as the inhabitants are in no rush, for today is their day of rest.

Opposite, at another cottage, a man emerges of indeterminate age wearing old trousers, a ragged pullover and a badly creased cap, which looks almost to be part of himself. He is tall but ever so slightly bent and he makes a sort of shuffle walk to reach a chicken run.

Those birds of his will not quieten until they are fed and they give the man no choice but to be up early, even on Sundays.

This man has done this chore for almost fifty years, and yet, this gives him just enough reason to carry on as before.

He is part of the village and is safe and sure as the stones and rocks which make up this sleepy and peaceful haven, well away from the rushing city life.

Newcomers and holiday people come and go, not making any significant changes to this tiny, obscure piece of the world.

This man, when young, had courted and wed a young girl from this same village. She had bright golden hair and she had been the light of his life. He was handsome and strong and could master a craft and turn his large brown hands to many other jobs too. He had never been without work.

An ingenious citizen he, like others from this place, had fought in the war and when he returned he found his children had grown as colourful as his vegetable patch.

His wife for fifty years has now gone and his children too . . . scattered to faraway places. He is now totally alone.

Each day is the same to this man now . . . only Sundays he recognises, as nothing changes for him in this quiet neck of the wood.

Coming with the sounds of Sunday . . . the silences and the peace, this is the time he allows himself to remember the life before. He gives thanks . . . there is nothing in this day that can disturb his reverie, nor a single thing which could salve the heaviness of his heart and his innermost yearning.

Not for one moment does he ever have an idea at all of the true value of his own worth . . . and sadly, there is no-one here left to tell him.

A NEW LIGHT
Clive Cornwall

The scent of wallflowers drifted lightly upon the warm air of the May evening. Old Mrs McGregor, rug around her knees, sat in her wheelchair, just inside the French doors at the rear of the house. The cottage was as nice as the evening, but the old woman kept fretting, as always.

She was worried about her son who was somewhere in France. He was a fighter pilot who flew from a makeshift airport, somewhere by a chateau in the south.

The old woman was restless. 'Nurse, nurse, where are you?'

Rosemary Cooke was a jolly girl who had nursed throughout the war and now spent part of her working life, which was most of it, nursing the old woman.

'Nurse, nurse, where are you girl?'

Nurse Cooke appeared through the doorway carrying a tray with a cool drink and various other potions upon it.

'Yes, Mrs McGregor, you called!'

'I certainly did nurse. Kindly remove that insect from the curtain.'

'Yes, Mrs McGregor.'

Nurse Cooke removed a pollen-drunk bee from one of the drapes and released it to the freedom of the evening air.

'Have you heard from Mr Hamilton?' the old lady enquired of her nurse.

'No, Mrs McGregor. No. It is nearly three weeks now. Nothing.'

'It's awful kind of you to write to my son, nurse. Of course, you realise that nothing can come of your friendship with Mr Hamilton when he returns, if he returns.'

Rosemary Cooke did not reply, but made the old woman comfortable and withdrew from the room.

A letter did arrive, next morning, informing Mrs McGregor that her son had received severe burns when his aircraft had been hit and brought down.

Rosemary continued to write over the months that followed, but did not tell the old woman that each letter received back was in a strange handwriting, and not always the same.

Then came the dew-clad mornings of late summer and with them a letter informing Mrs McGregor that her son, Flt Lt Hamilton Chaucer McGregor was coming home.

The old woman fussed and Nurse Cooke made preparations for the 'hero's' welcome home. And then, suddenly, the war was over. Mr Hamilton would marry the girl he'd once become engaged to, Miss Fiona Stewart.

Miss Stewart came to the house on a golden October day, but did not stay and it was Rosemary Cooke who was left to speak the necessary words of comfort to the man surrounded by darkness for, you see, Miss Stewart did not wish to marry a blind man whose face still bore the tender scars of sacrifice.

'She will return. She will return. It was a shock for her.'

Rosemary Cooke agreed with the old woman, but knew differently in her heart. If only the old woman lived until May of the following year, she could have seen her son, Mr Hamilton, come alive again in the arms of Rosemary Cooke, the girl he married on a day warm with the scent of wallflowers.

'Oh look!' cried one of the guests, 'There's a bee on your bouquet.'

And so there was. Rosemary smiled and so did Hamilton as a new light came into his life.